MIRRORS: HOLDING THE VISION

Book IV

The Accounts
of a Pleiadian Traveler

Nakala Akasie

Point of Light Pleiadian Publishing

ISBN: 978-1-942445-06-7
(e) ISBN: 978-1-942445-07-4

Library of Congress Control Number:
2016936611

Printed in the United States of America
10 9 8 7 6 5 4 3 2 1

Cover designer: Marsha Slomowitz
Typographer: Marsha Slomowitz
eBook: Marcia Breece

CONTENTS

ACKNOWLEDGEMENTS

I wish to thank my best friend and husband for his unwavering support of my work as a Pleiadian Messenger and Author.

*We come down to bestow upon you the Heavenly Spirit
and the multitude of gifts that can't be seen with
your physical eyes. Behold what cometh unto you,
the energy of pure love. This energy is of the highest
vibration known. When you ask or give to another,
you always receive in abundance.*

~THE AKASIE

*

The Voice

Let it be said: Today I place my focus on what
I want—not what I have had in the past.

This is how new momentums are created—
how Heaven on Earth is created.

We as a collective must create our own world together.

This is ours to do.

This is written as law.

As with any new craft there will be a period of practice to envelope the grand scope of it all. Look into the mirror. See yourself—see your fellow man. Set your intention on perfection. Manifest Heaven on Earth. Hold the vision. Become One with it.

~NATHANAL AKASIE

INTRODUCTION

By The Akasie

Life is a gift as these interactions—these communications—the guidance that you receive from the unseen realms are.

We the Masters of the family of Akasie from the star nation of Pleiades have come for you, to assist you in learning about your true self—your God-Self. We desire greatly that you also learn about the Ego Self the one who has taken control of many aspects of your lives. We desire greatly to show you the way through our many methods of guidance. This book is merely one.

PART

ONE

MASTER WRITER
BABARÓ

CHAPTER
ONE

My computer screen remained stark white except for the tool bar at the very top. I squinted my eyes, as I stared at it, half-way expecting the words to just appear by themselves. Just moments previously, I had heard that we were to begin our next book. But the words I had received made no logical sense at all. Then came absolute silence. I did not hear anyone dictating to me… No message was coming through. Nothing at all.

After a few moments of waiting for Babaró to get on with it and begin his dictation I heard a series of words that were unclear—garbled. I replayed the words in my mind working to decipher them, but no matter how many times I repeated them they hadn't made a bit of sense, so I had decided not to type them. Then distinctly I heard the words, "Royal Treatment." A sense of frustration pervaded and then my logical mind took command. With conviction I had said out loud to *myself*… knowing full well Babaró, my spiritual guide, who is in charge of the books I channel, was listening, "You are just wasting your time sitting here waiting!"

However, in the very next moment, I pushed aside my anxiety, sat up straight, and began to breathe deeply—purposefully to free my mind of all thought and expectation as I waited for Babaró to take over.

Just minutes before, I had been surprised and thrilled that Babaró had announced earlier that our last book in the series we were working on, *In The Light of Day, Book III* was finished—complete. The ending had come swiftly—unexpectedly. Physically, I had not risen in celebration or even in acknowledgement of our achievement.

However, I had assumed—hoped—that I would have some time to do something fun.

Not receiving clear guidance, I started to put away my small stack of notes and pencils and further tidy up my desk as I waited for Babaró to say something—to do something.

The book we had finished had taken us months to get through. It would seem to me, logically, that perhaps we would take some time off from writing—maybe go out to dinner—watch a flick perhaps.

Instead, Babaró had not hesitated taking me swiftly to the next book—this book. It was still early in the afternoon, and it looked to me as if Babaró had a well-defined agenda—a goal that he aspired to. I sighed wondering what Babaró had in mind—why he pushed me so hard.

I went back to the statement, "Royal Treatment" that had been delivered void of emotion. There was no way I could accurately interpret the meaning; but I sat with it contemplating the implication of the words, nevertheless. Was the intention behind it meant to test me—to see if beginning a new volume so quickly might ruffle my feathers? Umm, it did make me wonder. I had expected that I would receive some time off. Certainly I figured I had earned it.

Was the person behind the words, "Royal Treatment", being sarcastic? I did not know how it was meant and because no other explanation had been offered. I simply had trusted Babaró Akasie. I mused, as he is the main guide who gives me the dictation—the words that go into my books. Because of that I decided to wait and see what would happen.

A few years back, I had begun to work with Quem, my Pleiadian father. Because of Quem's vast authority he had many responsibilities and had delegated the teachings and writing to others who were members of Telbar who were chosen to assist me in my ascension to become an ascended master. Babaró had agreed to stand in as the master writer. I had wanted Quem to continue his teachings—to work with me on the books. But that had not been his choice for various reasons. I knew this was to be for now.

It has been several years since I first heard the name Babaró uttered. I would expect that after all this time I would know him intimately, but that hasn't been the case at all.

Truly I can compare him with a school teacher who never reveals his personal activities, only teaches the required curriculum. It seems what little he has revealed has been for the sole purpose of using it as a teaching tool—to assist me with my lessons. Babaró took over as head master after our book, *When Angels Speak,* was released. I felt he must be a very private person, because, still after all of these years, I knew very little about his activities other than he is here to assist me with the books!

Understand, please, that the spiritual guides telepathically speak to me and through me. They are writing the book through me using some of my most intimate experiences. They also project different ideas and scenes (visions) to assist me with the writing—to expand the teaching in certain chapters.

Because the books are meant to assist me in a variety of ways: one being to learn to recognize which of my beliefs are really hang-ups that have prevented me from growing in certain areas and working through them. To engage me fully, I am encouraged to participate in dialogue in the books by responding to their comments or teachings in my own authentic voice. This shows me what my true thoughts and feelings are concerning any given subject which ultimately reaches deep into the subtle layer of my consciousness of which I have little or no memory.

It has only been a few days since Babaró revealed what I consider to be one of his inner-most secrets. What is his secret? He lived on the Earth during the 1800's as the famous American poet, Henry Wadsworth Longfellow. Well, I am still processing that information. To me it seemed that this information would have been nice to know. For him to not share it, told me that the information was guarded—personal—wasn't for just anyone. The information was controversial, and, of course, I speculated about it for a long time. Being detail oriented, I of course, examined every angle of his disclosure with great care and consideration looking for flaws, discrepancies. I simply didn't know what to make of it as I was sure the disclosure was partial—incomplete. So I waited.

I didn't have to wait long as the very evening of Babaró's announcement I had gone to a Violet Flame Decree Group in Mt. Shasta and had learned that Mark Prophet of The Summit Lighthouse (a spiritual organization) had claimed to have been Longfellow in a previous embodiment as well.

(Mark had passed in 1973.) My present understanding is two souls do not incarnate in the same body at the same time! So how could this be that Babaró and Mark had the same life—shared the same body?

After Mark's transition he took his ascension and now is the Ascended Master Lanello.

For Babaró to reveal that type information on the very day that I go to a decree group and hear a similar tale just wasn't cool. Disappointment and doubt had made its way into my heart. Why did this happen? Why would Babaró tell me such a thing if it weren't true? He had assured me that what he said was the absolute truth!

Presently, I have not gained the final understanding of Babaró's story. Wondering if I should include any more explanation concerning this *adventure* of Babaró's, I reexamined the details as I knew them and came to a very strong conclusion that since this information was included in the last book, *In the Light of Day: Book III* of this series and in print I should expand on the teaching.

I wonder if this is some sort of error: did I get the wrong message? How many other times has someone claimed to have embodied as a particular person and have another make the same claim?

Because of my own experience as a channel, I ponder the possibilities. Perhaps there is more to the story? Could it be possible that two souls may unite and embody on Earth in the same physical body to achieve a greater momentum or contribution to mankind? This is certainly all food for thought.

Before this Longfellow story emerged, it never occurred to me that Babaró had lived on the Earth plane, much less lived such a note-worthy life. Yet, for him to disclose this information to me and even have me put it in the last book I felt was, in part, an honor somehow: he trusted me on this level to discuss this part of his life's experiences—one of his past lives.

Never have I found that there is one single reason the guides will share any information. As I examined possible motives, I thought perhaps Babaró merely felt it a noteworthy subject to expand on. Maybe he had planned to give me the information to assist people through my experience. I really don't know though.

I am on a fence here, teetering. I have a powerful suspicion that possibly I should just keep quiet regarding Babaró's disclosure. I believe I have weighed all my options and see it highly possible that perhaps in this writing Babaró will give me the rest of the story.

To sum it up: I have come to know there is always a higher understanding, that there is always an ulterior motive—a multifaceted reason, in fact, that may be extremely complex to the point that I do not grasp the entire teaching right away. The guides, I have unmistakably noticed, parcel out information in a delicate but very deliberate manner, building upon it as I am ready for additional data. There is more coming; it is a matter of what and when.

✳ ✳ ✳

Since I began to channel the Beings of Light, my life has drastically changed—shifted—for the better. In the beginning of my awakening to this particular spiritual gift to communicate and channel there have been times that I was terrified. Every emotion had been felt; literally, I had been extremely vulnerable and raw. It came down to basic survival for a while. I was alone, new and inexperienced to working with the guides—understanding their ways of teaching.

Back then, I hadn't comprehended that the Beings of Light, who include ascended masters, the angelic realm (archangels), and spiritual guides had specialties and were totally committed to service to me. It had depended on my level of awareness…where I was in the scope of it all—how they could assist. There are universal laws in place that they must obey.

To make it clear, these Beings of Light work in particular areas by serving in specific ways according to the needs of the hour. The length of service has varied substantially, some staying beside me since the day I began to hear them telepathically. Others have worked with me for a few days, weeks or months. While there are others who come every several months to check in—the reason for this remains elusive to me. Additionally, there are the guides who remain in the background never disclosing their presence—invisible—anonymous. They have been giving me their support by radiating their love in times of sorrow and cheering me on as I became more open to receiving spiritual knowledge. Literally, they are in celebration when I achieve in any area.

With an exorbitant amount of patience, the Beings of Light waited for me to set my sights on aligning with God's Will: because it is by Divine right that I have free will to choose. My goal is to heal (reprogram my beliefs to be aligned with my I AM Presence (the God in me)). As I align with the totality of my God-Self—my individual Divine Cosmic Matrix—I will graduate from this Earth plane becoming an ascended master (lady master) myself.

Through the guidance and teachings I have received I have come to realize that I am working toward my ultimate target by serving people through the channeled books, spiritual teachings and readings, and by loving all of creation. As I travel my path I am to acknowledge and honor each life form and intelligence as a Sacred Divine Spark of our Living God. This is my Sacred Contract.

I had stopped to reflect on my feelings concerning my writings and channelings when I heard Babaró begin to speak, "The time is nigh for the people on the Earth plane to receive the sacred messages-teachings. The time is now for the people to expand their minds and their hearts to God's Laws—God's Truths. We are benevolent Beings of Light who have traveled the galactic highways far from our homes in order to assist you in the process of evolving; going higher into Light and Love.

"More members of the mass consciousness who make up the collective Divine Cosmic Matrix are awakening every moment—their lights are luminescent, expanding, and radiating in unprecedented waves and gradations as they remember their Divine Essence. For this acceleration of movement we are most grateful.

"Through you and others like you we are able to reach unfathomable numbers of beings. The energies you create: I speak of your love and gratitude as you receive the channeled communications are sent into the cosmos swirling and joining like energies, in a majestic magnetic dance traveling to the correct corridor it is distributed: gifted to the peoples on the Earth.

"Each moment, we create with the intention of celebration of creation. This is orchestrated in a number of avenues: writing the books as we do is but one. With the creation of the books there are numerous persons involved. Look closely. When someone—any of us think about the writings, speak of them, or when they are read by you or another, more energy is created and distributed to the cause—the intent. With each facet more energy is added to the cosmic mix, always expanding upward and outward to assist in God's Creation in the evolutionary process, or what we call The Procession. Can you not see it?"

As Babaró dictated his words, I had begun to envision the surface of the Earth. It was as if I were stationed far up in the night's sky having a full view of the entire landscape: every city, home, business, road, and highway. I could see the mountain ranges the valleys, the rivers and lakes. I saw the oceans. Everything was animated and twinkled. I had never seen anything so stunning. With the utmost of clarity, I could see the cosmic plumes of energy rising and swirling upward and outward from surface. I could see that more energy rose from the Earth's larger cities and less from the areas that were less populated into the starry night sky. However, as I looked more closely I saw that this was not always the case. There were a few places that no large city existed where vast columns of energy rose high up into the sky like they were magnetically pulled to certain swirls of energy. Fascinated, I watched the colorful energies continue their journey uniting with other clouds of energy making vast shapes of cosmic dust. The energy was iridescent—rainbow-like, and in places the colors were denser than in other places. It was a virtual kaleidoscope. For a while, Babaró stood back—silent as he allowed me to take witness of this exquisite cosmic dance before he picked up where he left off, "Can you see it? The lot of you are engaged in a magnificent procession of celebration. As you proceed on your journey you are awarded the star of excellence as God's marvelous individuals and collective expressions of Love and Light."

Babaró's words tripped me up. "What do you mean we are being awarded the star of excellence?"

At first it didn't seem that Babaró was going to address my question, instead he made a request, "If you could please shift your view of what you are doing at this time… You have taken on to label what we do together, specifically our writings, as *work*. The word itself denotes a labor intensive mission and in particular moments you conjure up the feelings of something tedious—heavy—strenuous even. We ask you to change your view-explanation of time spent on these endeavors and recognize the joy of it all. We are in celebration at this time as this what we do, together, is truly a blessing and what brings pleasure to our lives. To celebrate is descriptive word indicating that you are honoring someone's achievement and is to be a joyful, perhaps even a playful experience. Your choice of words is important, Dear One, as each word sets a tone—a pattern—painting a picture for your future to be viewed and amplified by all.

"Consider this: You are the mirror and because of this you are to hold the vision of God's Creation—Love and Light. I emphasize this: It is *God's Creation* that you are to hold the vision of…not *man's creation*. Everything you do is to be done in celebration to honor God's Immaculate Concept and His creation.

I felt my gratitude soar as I realized the enormity and the simplicity of Babaró's words. "Nakala, you feel with my last statement: "You are to hold the vision of God's creation" is an exemplification of life itself. No other words or explanation are warranted. I see that you are complete. All that is required to be complete and at peace throughout your journey is to be mindful of these words: Be in celebration each and every moment. What else can possibly make a difference? My statement was that profound and had made its mark deep in your heart. *To have this understanding, this attainment of awareness, is to have received the star of excellence.*"

I paused for several minutes reflecting on Babaró's teaching before I asked, "Seriously, Babaró, what more needs to be said? If everyone could take that statement and consciously apply it to their daily lives what else is necessary?"

"The fact is, Nakala, you were ready to receive that message and receive it you did! For eons there have been messages and teachings of that exact sort, and look at where the people are at this moment. People ascend at different times according to their level of consciousness. We must continue on to reach people in a variety of ways!"

CHAPTER
TWO

Another realm…another dream…I am a Pleiadian traveler. My soul seeks the wisdom of Spirit—God. My consciousness is infinite, always expanding—always seeking God's Truth—God's wisdom. I never stop.

The physical body must sleep in order to replenish—to restore itself; my consciousness does not. I am an intricate Being of Light, who, through the centuries of being, caught in the web of man's mistruths, turned away from my Creator, my God, the Source of all, and thus my Light dimmed somewhat. But it still shines; never to be extinguished. Never!

*   *   *

Earlier this week a new guide showed up here. Her name is Rebeka. At first, I thought her purpose was to assist me with my artwork. More specifically to channel through me the various sketches I wanted of the guides and ascended masters who I *work* with. There that word is again. I feel the heaviness in my body as I say it. It has remained there on my subtle level of consciousness like a self-imposed infraction waiting for the correct time to be released forever.

In the beginning of my channeling career, Tirclé a guide from the Akasie family (my sister in fact) had channeled several portraits through me. I had simply made myself available by relaxing in my recliner with a drawing pad in my lap and a soft-lead pencil in my hand and let her guide the pencil as I watched on. I had to be detached in order to get out of the way. She was an excellent artist. She gifted me with several pencil drawings of the Akasie members (Pleiadians), archangels and some other beings who were of Sirius.

In some of the portraits, Tirclé had added insignias to their clothing (or what appeared to be uniforms) in the appropriate places. At the time she said the badges indicated they were members of the Galactic Federation. Since then I have learned there are many various councils or committees and some beings serve on several councils at any given time. Some of the beings had very large almond shaped eyes and long necks. Most of the beings looked like humans except these two features that had seemed to be greatly exaggerated.

I have known about Rebeka for a short while and am anxious to get on with the drawings. Mostly, I am curious to see what my other guides look like. Although, maybe that isn't all that important…to know what they look like, that is.

Rebeka seems to be waiting for something. When I ask for her to speak, usually, I just feel my vibration go higher as if she desires communicating through emotion rather than words.

Below I have added two transmissions from Rebeka that caused me to question her real identity. You will see that her way of speaking isn't quite like mine or yours. It is a little choppy with some of connective words left out. The transmissions appear, to me, to be full of holes— leaving me to wonder what her *real* intention was.

TRANSMISSION ONE

Yes, I have spent days with you. Since last Sunday, yes? I have enjoyed my time. I am putting out the energy that I don't feel I am correct for position. But I will give it a few more days before I/we decide.

I will discuss more at later time. Just know I am trying out like a new glove to see how it feels. (I presumed she was referring to the artist position.)

The Sirius Council of Light put me here. I agree to head up a team to come together for project. Complex. I am currently assessing qualifications, skills, and etc. of each individual who has put in application for project.

I assess what the needs are in order to make project come together.

Rebeka never makes it clear what project she is referring to.

TRANSMISSION TWO

Nakala—Today has been an awe-inspiring day.

I will let you know by Saturday evening (tomorrow) what I decide concerning project.

I see you becoming more comfortable with my chosen modality of communication. It is best to allow the unfoldment to occur naturally. I understand you are a bit limited in your view. Know if you are not comfortable it is not natural. I take initiative *ALWAYS*.

We, (the group) are pleased you go to view the Yogananda movie (Awake: The Life of Yogananda.) It was motivational and inspiring. Perhaps you get back to your yoga practice? We believe you are ready to incorporate this discipline in your days once again. Begin with two times per week. Begin this Saturday and Wednesday.

Again, what project is she referring to exactly? By limited in my view Rebeka is acknowledging that I only know what I am told. When I visited Myra, Pleiades, I attended a meeting and signed an agreement written by the Sirian Council of Light to work on a book with them to celebrate the lives of thirteen elders. Is this the project Rebeka is referring to? (The meeting is written about in the book, The Sacred Contract: Book II.*)*

✳ ✳ ✳

Quite unexpectedly, Rebeka announced Friday, a day earlier than expected, that she was ready to give me the results of her findings and asked me to retrieve my personal journal to record her transmission.

The Sirius Council of Light has given me the go-ahead to give you my decision concerning the project mentioned beforehand.

I have reviewed the case and have enough information gathered to have my say.

There are many beings who are agreeable to celebrate God's creation through the written text-your/our books.

I have carefully and thoroughly examined all applicants who have, on a higher level, agreed to gift humanity with their skill or support in any area, be it on the physical level or another level through the book(s).

The project is complex-taking many steps to complete. The project is the book we agreed upon; in celebration of the thirteen elders.

You have a vision in mind of the finished product. The book is striking in its quality, design, and prose! In full color there are portraits of each elder included.

Of course an artist is required and has been secured. We have chosen all peoples who are to contribute to the aforesaid project. All are agreeable to the contract.

I speak of the Higher Selves of those who reside on the Earth plane. The Higher Selves are to communicate with their lower conscious awareness. I speak of those who have awakened and are skilled in a specific area that they may collaborate with you on the project at hand. The lower consciousness must listen to the heart (the three-fold flame) in order to answer the call to complete the contract.

Remember you have been given free will. This is part of the lessons given to attain higher levels of enlightenment.

You see, I was assessing people who are skilled on the Earth plane not those of the Higher Realms. I know precisely who are to assist you and in what areas to complete the project.

You are to go forward in your writings. When it is in alignment to do so we will begin the book the Sirius Council of Light has contracted out to the committee of Comterous…you.

It is understood that you, Nakala, have several works in progress just now.

Allow the process to go naturally. From us, there is absolutely no need or desire by us for you to be assertive in any part of the creation of the book(s).

I am not your artist. An artist, grand, from the Sirius team will come your way and gift you with the paintings. No, do not think of the Sirius team as separate or other entity. We have come together uniting for the good of mankind. When I speak of team Sirius it is because I want you to know that we are contributing, as well, to this endeavor…not just the Comterous. (Comterous is a Pleiadian group formed to bridge the Higher Realms to the Lower Realms for purpose of multimedia—communications.)

In the last transmission I noticed twice Rebeka had used a plural connotation for book. Is this an error or possibly a clue that there may be more than one book to come? No answer has been given.

"Babaró here, Nakala. It is quite a pleasant surprise to receive Rebeka's review today instead of having to wait until Saturday (tomorrow). This frees you up somewhat for the weekend."

"Babaró," I began, "I really didn't understand Rebeka's statement, quote, 'I am putting out the energy that I don't feel I am correct for the position.' None of that made any sense to me. Will someone explain this to me please?"

I waited for Babaró to explain because I thought Rebeka was no longer here. She had given her report to me and I felt that was that. To have them just vanish after a transmission without saying goodbye isn't at all unusual.

Instead, I heard Rebeka say, "I speak for myself. This is Rebeka. Always, you are being stretched-primed for times ahead. I purposefully played the part that I was in turmoil and was surmising my options very carefully. I purposefully put on airs that I wasn't sure I wanted to work with you. This was to check your level of anxiety and feelings of attachment/detachment concerning working with me or other Beings of Light. It boils down to this: your thoughts and feelings of worthiness (belief of) and allowing God to work through you when all is in alignment to do so. You did react to my statement but were able to work through it with speed and accuracy. This is why I decided to give you my findings early. You had released all attachment to the project even though you weren't sure what the project was. You see, part of this was my choice to be evasive as a teaching. This in itself may cause reaction—the ego's need to know what is occurring on all fronts. This is about your need to control the outcome."

PART
TWO

A VISIT FROM
ISHMAEL TEAM SIRIUS

AND

THE HIGH PRIEST ADAMA
OF TELOS

CHAPTER
THREE

It wasn't long after Rebeka had left my home that a group had arrived and said, "We want to give you words just now."

Last night I had just finished watching the movie entitled, *Séraphine* about a common French housekeeper who painted at night by candle light. I had been able to easily identify with the movie because it was suggested that her guardian angel actually guided Séraphine's hand (painted through her).

Séraphine de Senlis 1864-1942 was a self-taught artist of the naïve style during the World War I era who was discovered by the avid German art collector, dealer, author and critic Wilhem Uhde. Wilhem also discovered other great contributors to our artistic world such as Picasso and Rousseau. Wilhem took Séraphine under his wing, as it were, encouraging her, buying her paintings and also by giving her advance payments on her work. She had been able to quit her housekeeping position and move into a larger apartment so she had space to paint.

Before Séraphine had been discovered by Wilhhem it was clearly portrayed that she was obsessed with her painting choosing to purchase art supplies with her meager wages instead of her paying her rent.

In the last years of Séraphine's life, she seemed to have lost her passion for life—her reason—her sanity and ended up in an asylum for the remainder of her years. Even with this unfortunate ending her work (or celebration of creation) became world renowned.

I find it clever that my guides maneuver me toward particular material for teaching purposes. This film was no exception as I was clearly guided to watch it as now I am clearly guided to write about it.

Babaró announced himself, "Nakala. Yes, I have been working through you in the brief synopsis of the movie, *Séraphine*, for purpose to inform the reader that there are oft times when an open channel, such as Séraphine, tips the scale, so to speak, not able to fully discern what is acceptable behavior in society. But perhaps, it isn't really about discerning acceptable behavior but discerning which reality she is in. Because of this Séraphine was deemed unstable.

"Séraphine was to channel her quote, 'guardian angel' or guide's artistic expression in order to assist not only Séraphine in her spiritual growth but to guide humanity through a shift in artistic impression. Séraphine had given herself over to her guide eagerly and to the point of becoming obsessive with her painting sessions causing an imbalance of sorts.

"Séraphine said her guardian angel told her to buy a wedding gown and wear it through town as she stopped at each home and leaving pieces of silver (candle sticks and tableware) on the door steps. It was then that the community called in the authorities accessing her behaviors as lunacy—she had lost her reasoning.

"We will get back to the film later," Babaró stated. "For now you have group waiting to speak to you." The group consisted of Stephanó, Franklin, Babaró, Sakeem, Nathanal and Ishmael.

The group's transmission:

We are here with you tonight. The movie and main character entitled the same. Séraphine was a real person who experienced telepathic communications from her guidance/spirit.

This guidance painted through her using Séraphine's hand. This is a walk-in or what some people refer to as over-lighting.

You are to understand that this is what you are experiencing as well. We wish to make it known that there are ones who wish to channel art/paintings through you.

Yes, we can be more specific. You are to have area (room) where you can paint. You are to finish all projects that you have started. No more are you to begin. Finish the beaded handle for the smudge feather. The knitting that you engage in, we do not consider this to be a project but an activity to relax with after your day of writing.

You have a patio area to set up an easel. We will watch for coupons and sales for supplies to assist in this endeavor.

The transmission took me by surprise. Before there had been communications indicating that I would do the portraits myself for the upcoming book that I had contracted with the Sirians. At length, I had explained that I didn't have any formal training as a portrait artist and felt I was not skilled as a painter and certainly did not have an aptitude for oil painting at all. (I talked to the guides as though they didn't have any knowledge of my past or my abilities.)

Having dabbled in oil painting at a young age, I had concluded that I was too messy when it came to this medium as I always managed to get paint on my clothes.

To the guides, it didn't seem to matter what I thought or what I said. Evidently, someone was eager to paint through me. No matter, I thought all of this will surely wait until next summer.

I noticed that a new name, Ishmael, (to me) had been added to the group's attendance list who had given the transmission. I had never had this guide come and speak to me. Because of this I wanted to get to know him, where he was from and his function in the group. Maybe he was a visitor or a student learning the ropes or someone who was observing for some reason or another.

After the group had completed the transmission, I had asked if they were leaving. (I knew Nathanal, Babaró, and Sakeem would be staying as they are my *personal* guides.) Nathanal is my twin flame overseeing my daily functions rarely leaving my side.

Stephanó and Franklin were doctors and part of the team Telbar and usually don't stay to visit.

Candidly, I asked if Stephanó and Franklin would be staying for a while. Stephanó answered, "Yes, Franklin and I have assessments and activations to execute tonight. Please make yourself available."

That left Ishmael. I began to attempt a dialogue with Ishmael by asking, "Ishmael, why are you here? Are you a student who is visiting?"

I was surprised that Ishmael responded so quickly. He began by saying, "I am of the Sirius Team. I find myself enthralled by the human apparatus." I was pulled in by his odd choice of words. This had engaged me—pulled me into conversation. I responded with, "I don't know why. You are much like us." (Although, as I said it I realized I had no real idea how *alike* we were and was embarrassed I had spoken without thinking.)

Ishmael's response was, "In some respects, yes, we are alike—but in others, vaguely similar. You vibrate at a much lower rate. For your species to accomplish any task seems to take extraordinary effort. Your focus—to maintain must be unwavering. To attain said *focus* under circumstances, for you, is quite crude—archaic even." (Ishmael was referring to the fact that our vibration wasn't high enough to sustain the adequate focus to accomplish complex tasks…rudimentary even.) "To get my point across," In a sure voice, Ishmael stated, "you haven't evolved to the level we have."

"At any rate, I appreciate your efforts—your design, like perhaps you appreciate a vintage car. You see?"

I didn't interrupt him but I realized that he was describing humans as being old-school. Okay, I get it. I almost felt insulted. But then his following remark could have been taken as an attempt at flattery so I just let it go. Perhaps he just didn't know how to talk in a socially acceptable manner or perhaps he was working to push my buttons.

Then Ishmael added, "There is much beauty to behold in the creation no matter the model or year." Inwardly, I thought well that sounded more like a compliment—sort of.

"The book you ask about—how you are to organize the data so it will be assembled with ease." He then channeled a deep breath through me reminding me to relax.

"Yes, I am team member—Sirius who works directly with Comterous to create 'packages' for distribution to further our cause.

"The book is of the thirteen elders but is not at all what you have imagined in your mind."

At that precise moment I knew what they had planned and I began to get excited! But at the same time I was confused because I had been given a clear picture of what the book was to look like. Perhaps they had changed their agenda?

Ishmael didn't describe the book with words. Instead, I received clarity (a knowing) on the mental level of what the book would be like. Still, I said nothing.

Ishmael continued, "The book is a novel with characters interwoven to accomplish grand task on Earth. No paintings are required except for the jacket cover. You can accomplish this can you not?"

This time I thought about it before I responded. "Well, one jacket cover is a far cry from thirteen portraits of masters I have never seen before. But it still depends on what you want as a cover—it is your choice to either have a painting created with oils or another medium or have a cover created by a graphic artist on the computer."

Ishmael continued, "I can tell you we are pleased you have held onto the ride—enjoyed—persevered—accomplished! We were in wait to see what you would do before we approached you and gave forth any further information concerning this project." As if his explanation weren't sufficient, he said, "We have monitored your progress. We are ready to proceed."

Ishmael continued, "After the third volume of the Pleiadian Traveler is complete we will channel the next book which is a Sirian collaboration."

"We are excited to work with you. We *know* you will continue forth in this area of writing as it creates a big stir in the heart…your heart."

I was in total agreement with what Ishmael said but didn't say so out loud. I knew that he was reading my aura.

During his communication I had formulated some questions. Perhaps he would be willing to answer them. I began by asking, "Who will channel the book—one person or a group?"

"I will." Ishmael answered not revealing any emotion.

Off the cuff, I made the comment, "It is a lot of work."

"I love it." Ishmael said still not betraying any feeling on the matter.

I shook my head in agreement and said, "As I do."

"We will get on together as if we are two halves of the sun—blazing together as one."

I chuckled. At that point, my heart quickened and I realized this one was a poet. Impromptu, I made a remark that surprised me. "Nathanal you'd better watch out for this one as he has a silver tongue."

Ishmael didn't comment on my parody but instead stated in a matter-of-fact way, "I like to write. There is no doubt. I wouldn't have taken on this project had I not."

I thought he had left me to my thoughts when I heard a sound like he was scooting a chair out from a table. What he did was highly unusual and quickly caught my attention. I looked in the direction where the noise had come from and connected to the energy to check if I could sense anyone there. At first, I didn't get any hits. Then I scanned the area closer to where I sat. There he stood directly before me. I raised my eyebrows as I looked up using my inner sight to see who this was.

I saw a tall being, slender with blond hair. Adama's image came to the forefront. I asked, "What are you doing? I see Adama the high priest of Telos, Mt. Shasta, California." I shook my head working to dislodge the image that I felt was sure to be incorrect. The image persisted to the point of becoming intrusive and even troubling. Someone channeled a deep breath through me. Still the image would not go away!

I gave in and said, "Okay Adama. Obviously you want to make yourself known." As if going into prayer I placed my hands together if front of my heart and bowed. All of this was done automatically. I questioned what was happening. I was taken out of my comfort zone as no formal announcements in advance had been made that Adama would be arriving today—now. I felt my vibration rise and became a bit light-headed. I began to do cleansing breaths. I considered going outdoors to get some fresh air—then thought about how cold it was out there. Disregarding that minor inconvenience I got up and stepped outdoors for a few minutes to clear my head, concluding that getting some fresh air would erase the image of Adama and bring everything back to normal.

But it was not to be. As I walked back in my office, in my mind's eye, I saw Adama sitting in my emerald green wingback recliner. Oh, Lord, I sighed. I felt like the image of Adama was a projection—not really him. Again, I shook my head to free the image and asked, "Okay, who is sitting in my chair?"

Hearing Babaró answer was somewhat comforting, "Honey," he began, "relax this is normal." Nervously, I laughed and exclaimed, "It may be normal for you! Not for me!"

Without responding Babaró motioned for me to sit and take dictation at my desk.

"Nakala, it was decided upon one month past that Adama would be in collaboration with you on the writings. Why does this visit trouble you so?" I felt my vibration rise again from the love the Beings of Light radiated completely contradicting with how I felt: I was not worthy to receive teachings from the Adama, the High Priest of Telso. I knew that this was another layer of that same belief that I was not good enough to associate with or receive from certain people who held high positions in the cosmos. I remembered when I had felt the same way about Jesus.

Then suddenly I realized that my ego had taken control of my thoughts and feelings. As quickly as I realized what had taken place the feelings of unworthiness were released. In its place an authority-a powerful knowing rose up in me. I said, "This is preposterous! I have work to do!" I took note of the shift in my energy: my feelings of doubt instantly subsided as I continued, "These transmissions are to take place in order to assist in the ascension of not only man but for all life forms and intelligences. I am one of the chosen scribes and I am honored to write your words for others to learn from."

Adama acknowledged my words by saying, "Thank you. Thank you very much. Let us begin."

"It has been just a few weeks ago that I came to you and you wrote my words for your last book, *In the Light of Day.* Yet after working with me several days you still felt that my arrival couldn't be so. That another had *projected* my image."

Yes, Adama was correct that I had felt unsure of what I was getting. I tried to explain, "I feel that because I am not seeing you as a whole—the details that make up your essence—that is what makes me wonder if I am really channeling you or perhaps someone else. I do not want *ever* to be inaccurate on who I am channeling *ever!*"

"Nakala, you were summoned to come to Mt. Shasta to work with us. Sakeem who works with us has been stationed in Telos for years, as

Jonson and Tabitha have and a host of others who are affiliated with us. I am devoted friends with your Pleiadian family—your mother, Sarah and father, Quem. Your parents asked me specifically to watch over you while they were away. While I do not personally come to your home and view your movements, Sakeem and the other guides who are ever-vigilant and based in your sphere on my behalf would most assuredly and respectfully report anything worthwhile to me or one of my noble associates.

"Let us continue?"

I sighed and said, "Yes, I am ready." Adama nodded his head once and began his dictation, "I wish to explain why you feel a bit overcome with my arrival. You have the personality that does better to 'ease into' transition—of any sort. This includes having *company*. To be told in advance assists you in the shift."

"Well," I retorted, "it *is* customary to let someone know that you are planning to visit."

"Does it make a difference?" Adama's question had been steady; not a single hint of condemnation. Adama paused for several seconds as he waited for me to reflect on his point. "You were due to work on the writings today. Does it matter who you receive from? Expect the unexpected and be grateful for the abundance of gifts that are bestowed upon you.

"We are beginning our merge to the people who reside on the Earth's surface as you can see. The Lemurian descendants who have incarnated on the surface of the Earth are being revealed, acknowledged, and accepted as such on the Earth's surface. There are those who are channeling the Lemurians and those who are remembering their Lemurian ancestry—lives past—our ancient culture and even our language. Nakala, you as well, are remembering and speaking our native tongue."

Astonished I asked, "What? Oh? I thought I was channeling the Pleiadian language."

"Nakala, we come from the Pleiades. There are dialects many as the beings have been evolving individually and as a collective for thousands upon thousands of years. Don't get caught up in inconsistencies.

"Because we, in Telos, have lived in the same forms for hundreds of years our memories have stayed intact and our spiritual ability and expertise have accelerated above and beyond most all of those who reside on the surface of the planet. In other words, our spiritual growth has not had to be reactivated time and time again like you as you have shed the human—physicality. Fear not, as all of that—disease and so called death comes to a complete close for you very soon. You with your soul family are on your way to fulfilling your lessons on Earth and ascending to the fifth dimensional level or sphere of consciousness."

I felt myself growing weary and announced that I needed a moment or two to see to my needs. As I got up from my chair I said, "Adama, thank you for not giving up on me." Adama response was comforting, "I would never give up on you, Nakala. You have come here across the nation to be near us, to learn from us, and to also assist us. I am pleased to give forth my wisdom and God's truths."

Then I added, "And Adama I promise that I will not be shocked the next time you arrive."

As I walked into the kitchen to get a snack and reheat my tea I heard Adama say, "It is time I take my leave. Know that I will return in the days to come to revisit the teachings for this book. There are others who are sure to come as well."

PART
THREE

CRYSTAL'S FATHER'S ACCIDENT

MY TRIP TO IOWA

CHAPTER
FOUR

The holidays have arrived and with it I have been given several days off from writing with the masters. After two days, I was itching to get back to my desk and took a chance by asking if it were possible to go ahead and write anyway. I figured what the heck, I have several hours before Thanksgiving dinner would be ready to be served, why not ask? I had been intrigued with Babaró's passionate answer, "Absolutely not! Nakala, we all celebrate the holidays and for us to take a day or two or even longer from activities is important to us as well. We have our own personal lives apart from you. Yes, it is important—our endeavors. For now we desire and must have time to ourselves to purify, re-energize in order to carry forth our mission in all that we do as teachers, healers, peace makers, and comforters. We move energy, transmute energy. We amplify and radiate energy and in order to accomplish tasks we must be clear of energy that is of a lower sort. All of us—your assistants, this team, including you, must cleanse and reboot. We could not—would not—go forth in our celebration of life if we did not honor the decrees.

"During holidays such as Thanksgiving much energy—gratitude and love is created on the level of the third dimension. Many of you step into the roles as givers by assisting those who are less fortunate, not only, but you are sending up waves of appreciation and joy for what you have as you once again are gifted in the coming together with family and friends for the holiday of Thanksgiving and partaking in the traditional meal.

"We are in gratitude as well, amplifying this energy as we all have much to be grateful for."

CHAPTER

FIVE

Finally, I felt settled in my new home in Weed, California and was looking forward to winter. I had been envisioning being snowed-in—unable to leave the house for a few days. Of course I had all of the provisions I required to make me comfortable. I saw myself looking out the frosty-cold windows and watching the animals forage in the deep snow for their buried treasures. The tree branches of the cedars, pines, and spruce trees were heavily laden with fresh white powder, like white scalloped frosting on a wedding cake. As the wind blew I saw the snow take flight and catch the sun's rays in a crystalized dance. The branches were bending down low from the accumulated weight of the snow to join the Earth in a ritual of thanksgiving. It was as if the trees themselves were providing shelter for the plant and animal life. This ritual is of the purest sort only taking place in the winter when all is laid to rest.

Like a young child, I anticipated putting on my snow pants and boots and looking through my winter coats to find the perfect water-proof coat I had. I saw myself sorting through my hats, scarves and gloves to pick out what would be the warmest and driest before I stepped out into the attached garage to get my snow shovel. I could feel the excitement—the newness of it all. As if opening gigantic curtains before a performance at the theater I pushed the button that opened the garage door to reveal winter's wonderland filled with treasure. The snow being a dazzling pure white refracted the sun's light: it sparkled like billions of tiny iridescent crystals that almost hurt my eyes. My chest expanded as I took in a deep breath. I saw my breath turn to a vapor as I let out deep inhalations in the cold crisp air. Like a child I laughed out loud as the joy overtook me.

Hurriedly, I saw myself walk outdoors in the snow and take notice of my foot prints. I wanted to find the area that was the deepest so I could lie down on the jewel laden earth that sparkled like rainbow prisms to make snow angels.

After I had created dozens of snow angels, I imagined myself taking fists full of snow and rolling them into giant balls to build a real snow man or woman—one with coal-black eyes, a carrot nose, and rocks for a mouth. I wanted to find an old flannel shirt or an apron and dress it to make it more real. This was the first year I felt like I could take the time and have fun! Most of all, I wanted to walk down the street and hear my footsteps crunch under my weight in the complete silence.

All of my dreams of playing in the snow had vanished in one clear-cut moment. No longer high were they on my priority list when my Pleiadian sister, Crystal had called me from Iowa to inform me of her father, Henry's near fatal car crash.

Crystal works with the Beings of Light: ascended masters, archangels, and spiritual guides. She is a healer and channel as well. As with all individuals she has her own unique way in how she communicates with the Higher Realms. Every week we try to connect and talk on the phone to catch up on the teachings we have had and our life in general.

Crystal's father, Henry, was in bad shape and required surgery. The family was receiving inconsistent reports from the doctors on staff concerning his condition. While one doctor reported that Henry had several fractures in his pelvic and neck area the next doctor informed the family that he didn't have any detectable fractures. One doctor had stated that Henry had a lacerated spleen and punctured bowel and collapsed lungs. Each doctor seemed to have his own version of Henry's injuries.

I felt a powerful urge to pack my things and get in my car and drive to them.

As Crystal explained the situation, I heard no emotion in her voice: she was what I call flat lining. She was on hyper drive—not feeling but doing whatever was necessary to see that her father receive the proper care. She was acutely aware that this may be her father's time to exit from the physical plane.

I knew at one point the emotions that she didn't feel (because she needed to stay present and make decisions) would emerge at a later time.

Unfortunately, by Crystal being the sole caregiver for both her parents on top of maintaining the household she was faced with a tremendous set of responsibilities. To a small extent I could imagine what she was going through as I had dealt with a similar situation with my parents.

I knew to go to Iowa wouldn't be a simple trek. To get to them would take me two thousand miles and an estimated five days of travel. For some unexplained reason I didn't want to fly.

On the phone I had explained to Crystal that I wanted to come and help her. Before any consideration, she immediately refused my offer saying that it was much too far for me to travel. Still my feelings persisted and the next time I talked to her I repeated my desire. I waited for Crystal to say, "Yes! Please come. I really could use your help."

The Friday after the wreck—the day that I left my home for Iowa, Crystal still hadn't said yes, come, but I had packed my bags anyway. I was nearly ready to walk out the door when I called and told her once again that I wanted to come help her. I said, "Crystal you have to ask me before I can come." That is when she had broken down and cried and said, "Yes."

As soon as I got the go-ahead, I loaded my bags in the back of Sarah Jane Blue, my Rav4, and headed out. My guides were planning my route and it wasn't thirty minutes into the drive that I shook my head as I questioned their first choice. Instead of staying on a four-lane highway they took me through a national forest on a two lane highway. You can imagine since I was in the mountains that the road was constantly curving, with steep inclines and descents. My trip had begun late in the afternoon and through the thick of the trees the sun began its fall less than two hours into my drive.

The darkness began to seep through the trees camouflaging the land and my ability to see clearly. As I drove southeast huge wet snowflakes began to fall hitting the windshield with astonishing force. My head lights and windshield wipers were on. The snow was falling so fast that the accumulation quickly exceeded three inches on the road. Needless to say, I was concerned about the driving conditions. There were no places to pull over and no places to stop for the night. Having no alternative, except to turn around or keep going, I drove on, adjusting my speed every few minutes as the slush began to pile up making deep, wet, soggy ruts in the road.

Soon it became apparent that I couldn't see well enough to be safe. I thought about on-coming traffic and wildlife getting in my lane and me not being able to see them fast enough to stop. I prayed to God to keep me safe and then I asked what I should do. Babaró's advised, "If I were you I'd turn around." He didn't have to tell me twice. Immediately, I did a four-point turn driving back the way I had come for approximately ten miles.

Then I saw it: the snow plow! Instantly, I found myself turning around directly behind it as the words came out of my mouth, "I am not going to give up that easily!" Intuitively, I knew that it hadn't been my lower consciousness who had formulated that thought and spoken through the physical body. However, in that singular moment I didn't have the time to examine the statement or who had said it. Onward I drove behind the plow through the storm until the snow let up and I found myself in a larger city and a place to stop for the night.

✳ ✳ ✳

The next day I woke up to a bitter cold coupled with gray clouds that looked as if the sky was severely burdened with a heavy load of snow. By then I felt I had invested too much time in this journey—too many miles to turn around and return home. I was now committed to this trip for the long haul. I set my mind on the positive by affirming that I would have clear blue skies and dry roads the entire trip and I believed it! But that wasn't to be. I ran into snow two more times before the roads cleared giving me the confidence to drive the posted speed limit.

On the fourth day of my travel, I was beginning to really feel worn out from sitting in my car and driving all day. I was more than ready to be finished with that part of my journey. In order to reach my final destination, however, I was looking at fourteen more hours in the car. I decided that it wouldn't be wise to push that hard. But as I drove on that night, I realized how close I was to arriving at my final destination and was suddenly spurred on. Every few moments I heard Babaró encourage me, "Keep going. You are almost there," until at last I drove into Crystal's small Iowa town and parked into her driveway.

CHAPTER
SIX

I was watching a Hallmark Christmas special on TV with Crystal and her mother, Joyce, when I heard someone begin to telepathically speak to me. He identified himself as Timberlund saying he was one of Crystal's guides.

Immediately, I speculated what an odd…even a preposterous name and who is this guy anyhow. However, after I examined the long string of unusual names I have heard since I began to work with the Beings of Light I surmised that his name wasn't really all that unreasonable and probably he had something of interest to share. So I focused on his words.

Timberlund said he had worked with Crystal for a long time but she was unaware of his presence. I wondered why he had kept silent—not introducing himself to her.

Talking with Crystal about this type of thing isn't guarded; there are no secrets between us that I am aware of. And I wasn't in the least concerned about speaking about these types of issues in the company of her mother, Joyce as she suffers from Alzheimer's. Joyce doesn't remember anything from one moment to the next. I waited for a commercial to come on before taking the opportunity to casually mention to Crystal, "We have another guide to add to our entourage." I saw Crystal's interest spike as she asked, "Who?"

"Timberlund."

As I answered I closely watched Crystal's facial expressions to gage her reaction or if she would even have one. At first, Crystal stopped to connect to her guidance then looked up at me and asked, "What kind of name is that?" I just shrugged my shoulders.

Her next comment was, "You know, I think he is Lemurian and wants to channel the Lemurian language through me."

Patiently, Timberlund waited—possibly for us to ask him some questions or perhaps for us to ask for him to talk to us.

As I talked with Crystal, I felt as if I had pushed the hold button on my phone for Timberlund's line as I talked on another line to Crystal except he could hear us. In a sense I felt as if I were being rude as I was quite aware that Timberlund was listening to every thought and word while he waited. I decided to go ahead and telepathically ask Timberlund if he was Lemurian? He answered, "Yes."

Then I asked, "Are you from Telos?" "Yes."

"Do you live in Telos?" "No, I live here now."

Then the TV show came back on and I redirected my attention to that. Again I felt like I was being a bit impolite to Timberlund but I did it anyway.

That night after I got into bed I was more than ready for some quiet time to relax, pray, and talk to my guides for a few minutes before I went to sleep. Sitting with Joyce is often disrupted as her thoughts get stuck and she will repeat the same question over and over. She constantly fidgets and picks at herself or objects. It takes an inordinate amount of energy and patience to deal with her. I was tired and wanted time to talk with my guides—to thank them without being distracted. I especially wanted to acknowledge all of what they do for me and all of humanity. When I began to thank my guides for their assistance today I heard someone say, "You are most welcome." I wasn't sure who had responded so I asked if it was Nathanal and I was told, "No, this is Babaró."

There are many times when I don't know who is speaking to me. Because I don't really hear the timber or tone of their voices unless I pay close attention to the little nuances that are presented: particular words or phrases that are spoken, the accent, gestures, or even an occasional image. All beings have a particular style of speaking or communicating—some being more distinct than others. I have found that some guides don't speak at all but are in waiting, or perhaps they give loving energy and assist in balancing our energetic bodies.

After I knew I was talking with Babaró I asked about Timberlund. Maybe I could talk to Babaró and find out why he had contacted me specifically.

After I said the name, Timberlund, I felt a shift in the energy—a different vibration and intuitively knew that Timberlund had come into my field. Timberlund didn't hesitate to speak to me at all and said, "Nakala, I have been here working with Crystal for many years. I have been waiting for a conscious connection between the two of us."

✳ ✳ ✳

Unintentionally, I had fallen asleep last night before my conversation with Timberlund was complete. I still had several questions still lingering on the periphery of my mind concerning Timberland.

This morning I was the first to rise. I readied myself as quietly as possible, made a pot of coffee and taking advantage of some private time I slipped into Crystal's office. I lit a candle and said a prayer and began to still myself before going forward with my day.

As I was sitting, I heard Timberlund announce himself and ask me to please pick up my journal as he had *words* for me. He began his teaching with, "You both, (Crystal and I), are able to see me to a certain degree. I have projected certain details of my body so you will question who I am. I am a Light Being just as your other guides are." Just then he showed me an image of his body. "However, as you can clearly see, my body is a little different looking than you are accustomed to. I showed you my height—I am to you a very tall individual with slender features (7'6"). My fingers are longer than most and I have connective tissue between my fingers making them look as if they are webbed. No, Nakala not like an amphibian just a bit of connective tissue. The pads of my fingertips, as are my toes, are highly sensitive and are larger than yours of the human race being designed to pick up or feel the energy-pattern or the signature of anything be it an article or a life force." (I knew there was much more to his abilities but for now that is all he was willing to disclose.)

"My creative expression is a bit different that yours. I sport a particular style of hair and fashion that you find most humorous even immature. For you, at least this eased my introduction a bit. Yet your belief is that since I have presented myself in this unusual attire this indicates that I am not *professional.* You question my sincerity, my authenticity, not only, but my worth as an ascended master! You are quick to judge are you not?"

"You call my chosen hair style 'punk' as I have selected the colors few to enhance my *groove.*"

I had focused on Timberlund's bleached hair. His hair wasn't particularly long but it was spiked and going in all directions. I did call his hair style "punk" as this is the same style that some of the kids and even older people were wearing these days. What I thought was particularly funny was this wave of hair on the top of his head that was hot pink and blue. His skin didn't have a healthy or ruddy color like us but was a stark white. I really couldn't see the details of his clothing but instead got an *impression* that he was wearing clothing (tight jeans and a jean jacket over two pullover shirts) that looked layered and mismatched with big bulky work boots.

Suddenly, because I didn't understand where this was going with Timberlund, I felt a little insecure and wanted some assistance from someone I knew. Timberlund wasn't my guide so why was he choosing to disclose his appearance to me like this? I felt like I wanted someone from my team to step in so I asked Samuel Paul, the Ascended Master I work with, to assist me.

Immediately, I was directed to look at the book shelf at two things— a drawing of a woman (specifically her eyes). Then the small air bubbles inside a round turquoise glass paperweight. The eyes meant to *see* or *look* and the bubbles inside the glass paperweight meant *within* or *inside.*

To look within or past what we see on the outside is what Timberlund was teaching. The old adage came to mind: You can't judge a book by its cover. I shook my head. Timberlund was correct. I had been quick to judge, and a swell of guilt settled in making itself known in an unpleasant way.

"Nakala," Timberlund said, "I appreciate your focus on this matter. This is a lesson: it would do you well to remember. All beings have a particular style or way of dressing. This is one way to express their artistic flavor—individuality. All people have the innate ability to express themselves by presenting or decorating the physical body not only (like with tattoos or jewelry) but with the clothing, how they carry themselves, and even how they speak.

"I have presented myself thus for purpose multifaceted."

"Of course," I muttered, "It always is…multifaceted, that is."

Timberlund continued his teaching, "I presented myself in an outrageous costume." I heard him chuckle under his breath. "This is my way of looking. This style is a statement…my statement that says I am having fun! I want to be different than the norm and let's just go crazy! Above all I am reaching beyond the average which can become quite tedious and even dull."

I wasn't sure how to respond because he used the word "crazy." I strongly felt that the word crazy could be taken as a negative connotation because we use that word to describe people who are not stable or grounded, and realized that it is exactly how I had judged Timberlund— as if he were unstable and ungrounded—a bit on the *crazy* side.

Immediately, I opened google on the Internet to look up the word "crazy" and realized that he was using it as a descriptive word that could mean wild, extreme, zany or a host of other meanings.

I knew that both Crystal and I had the preconceived idea or even opinion that the masters always wore loosely fitting white robes. I was fast realizing that quite possibly my perception of how the guides presented themselves may be completely wrong. What did *we* know about how the masters dressed?

Then I recalled one comment my Pleiadian father, Quem had made a while back. He said that he dressed according to the occasion. I supposed this said it all. I had to laugh. If you truly wanted to shake up a couple of middle-aged women who had traditional views, putting on a get-up like Timberlund had would certainly do the trick.

So what was this Timberlund really like? Was this all a show to wake us up and prove to us that we held certain prejudices? Could this be the way he really dressed as he guided Crystal? I thought about myself and how my style of dress had changed over the years. As a rule, I don't buy clothing that is particularly what I'd call 'fun'. What I buy is clothing that I'd consider practical but looks professional and nice enough that I could go out on a date or on a job interview. Wow, I hadn't thought about it but I guess I could be considered a little on the boring side.

Then out of left field I remembered a transmission I had been given before I came to Iowa to visit Crystal. Part of the transmission had been a message *for* Crystal. In other words they had wanted me to pass on the message! The message had been given to me during a meeting held by The Pleiadian Council of Light. The speaker was Jordan.

It isn't all that unusual to be given a message to pass on to someone else but with this particular message I hadn't wanted to get involved.

First the council went into prayer then covered some general business.

TRANSMISSION

"Now, we are all present, ready, and willing to go forth together as a whole—United as One.

"Nakala, we offer to you in celebration of God the position of scribe.

"You are aware that all we do is for purpose multifaceted."

As I had been receiving the transmission I had been a little distracted by something Crystal had just shared with me. I suspected that the memory was being projected by someone on my team for the sake of this transmission.

Late one night, after doing several healing sessions with a family, Crystal had been driving home at a fairly high speed on a dark, unfamiliar, country road.

Crystal had been flying high because she had forgotten an important protocol: to ground herself after each session. As she had sped down the gravel road she had been chatting on her cell phone, when she suddenly realized that there before her glared a stop sign and a sign that indicated there was a T in the road. She had to stop to turn either left or right but she had known instinctively that there wasn't enough time.

What she experienced next defied all logic. Crystal said the Ascended Masters who watch over her had shifted the hologram. She saw a wall or wave, if you will, of energy, like a time warp. The appearance of the wall was much like the heat that rises off of the asphalt of a hot road, only this energy you couldn't rightly see through. She had said that it had been as if time and space were not an issue—did not exist. The car did not slide to a screeching halt but merely had slowed a bit and turned to the left.

After the incident, she saw that there was a steep ravine on the other side of the T. Crystal had been upset over the incident but was so grateful for what these beings, whoever they were, did. She was positive that without the intervention she would have crashed. They had saved her life.

Crystal also had said that the conversation with her friend had never been broken—she had never let on what had happened—merely had continued the dialog. To this day her friend still doesn't have any knowledge of the episode.

As if on que, as soon as the memory of Crystal's story was complete, Jordan continued…

"Crystal is an officer, as you, and is to be at *all times* cognizant of her thoughts, emotions, and actions. This means being vigilant of the physical body's requirements—to keep safe.

"You both are learning (aware now) that in certain settings it is imperative that you be grounded in the physical body. You must listen to the bodies all to know what is required to stay balanced and safe. (There is more to this but for this teaching we are focused on thus.) This is to be accomplished through commands, breathing, and allowing the transition to take place. Not rushing to the next segment before all is in alignment.

"Again, I remind you of the fact: you are officers. As officers you must implement directives.

"These words are to be shared with Crystal. She has not yet picked up the pen to communicate with her guides in this manner." [Jordan meant she had not ever taken dictation from the masters.]

"Perhaps she will think on it. The channeled writing encourages integration of certain teachings.

"We have asked her to write repeatedly—conversation is to be had."

At that moment I curtly interrupted Jordan declaring, "I don't want to talk about Crystal or to her about this subject." Completely disregarding my statement Jordan continued on with his dictation.

"We see it as thus—everyone is a team member. Yes, you and Crystal, both, are part of our team. Certain efforts are to be made in order for the team to run smoothly—more efficiently.

"Officers don't go into the field and forget rules—forget protocol. This gets people killed. All must act responsibly—ALL."

At that Jordan announced, "We are adjourned."

I understood that Crystal had not followed protocol on two counts. She had not grounded herself after her sessions. Literally, she had been consciously elevated into a higher dimension. Then Crystal had driven down that blackened corridor while talking on the phone. She had not been fully present while she was driving.

Thank God there had been an intercession.

With all that had been presented a peculiar question nagged at me: how many times will the Beings of Light intervene if a person repeatedly disregards protocol?

* * *

At once I saw the complexity of the lesson I was receiving. I had been guided by my I AM Presence (my God-Self—my Higher Self—my higher mental body) to come to Iowa and assist my friend with her parents during this time. Crystal's mother was a handful. Then her father had the near fatal *accident*. (My guides say there are no accidents just misaligned energy.)

Crystal lives in a small community and has a fairly large family. Her parents have lived there for over sixty years and know everyone. Because of this Crystal felt that everyone should be kept informed of her father's status. (She felt as their caregiver this was her duty.) Because of this belief colorful stories of the accident and what the doctors said and did were being repeated to family and friends: virtually everyone who called to express their concern. I heard the stories breed like feral cats as they were repeated over and over. I shook my head and wondered how long I could continue listening and *feeling* without speaking my truth.

During my drive to Iowa Babaró had pointedly given me his direction regarding my, so-called, duties while I stayed at Crystal's home, "Nakala, you are to assist in the household tasks and errands. You are also to be a support person by *listening* to Crystal during this time as she will be processing and making decisions."

Two days after I arrived at Crystal's home she began to get a sore throat. Still I said nothing. I offered her Echinacea tea with lemon and honey. I prompted her to go to take naps—go to bed. I did the best I could without getting pushy or demanding. What was I to do? Some days she would feel better. As soon as she felt a little better she picked up her duties again which included her perceived duty to keep everyone in the loop.

At the time, I was not directed by Babaró or any of the other guides to speak my truth about the energy that was being created by the family members as they constantly retold the story of the wreck, how badly Henry had been hurt, and the blatant inconsistency of the diagnosis and prognosis of the doctors. Because I wasn't told to say anything I remained silent for several days watching the drama develop!

I am sitting here writing about the negativity that has been created surrounding that incident. As I assess what I am doing I realize that I am doing the same thing—creating negative energy. Emphatic, I proclaimed to my guides that I felt it wise to discontinue this line of writing and go back and delete what I had written.

However, before I had a chance to follow up on my announcement, I heard my name being called and my heart expanded. "Nakala, honey, this is Babaró. We have brought you here for a teaching that is grand—

a wealth of information for Crystal and you. Consequently, this information will spill outward affecting all of the mass consciousness. This teaching is extremely important. I wish that you not feel that through the writing process you are doing something incorrect to the extent of being harmful to mankind. This is not so. I am guiding you through this lesson in order for you to integrate it fully.

"I am your guardian and your master teacher. Remember that I only want what is best for you, and that is for you to learn to control your thoughts, emotions, and actions. You are here as an observer. This is true. However, because you are sisters who walk beside one another on the path of service it is for you to speak your truth with love.

"During the night we worked with the both of you on this subject of telling stories that are negative. Crystal is aware now of why she has taken on this cold. She is out of alignment with spirit and misused her voice. Therefore she is almost unable to speak.

"Yes, Henry had a run-in with another vehicle and was physically hurt. But I speak the truth. This is a grand scheme to assist the entire family in healing—to come together working as a fine-oiled machine for the common good of *family*.

"First things first, Nakala, yes the stories fly growing more sensational, or shall I describe them as bleak, with each retelling? You have been a bystander observing it all; chosen by your Higher Self to serve in this manner.

"As you see the drama unfold, you have witnessed many of the family members' egos on display: the need to be right, the need to save, and the need to be a perfect support person. Be it a daughter or son, granddaughter or grandson, another family member or even a friend, they have believed by showing their concern or even getting involved in some manner is the socially acceptable and the expected thing to do.

"You have seen sibling rivalry escalating. In other words, there has been a competition of sorts accelerating in momentum to gain favor from the injured party.

"The family has been frightened as well, that they will lose the patriarch of the family. Some expect his passing! Some, even on subtle levels, want him to pass; get on with it! He is, after all, near ninety years of age! Emotions have flared. People are acting and reacting. Some have given of themselves with much love while others hold back. You see it all unfolding. This is a grand teaching for you. We are pleased that you are witness and are asking, allowing, and accepting our assistance as you sort out and integrate the knowledge that, for you, will ultimately free you from bondage."

Babaró paused a moment. He sensed I had a question and waited for me to formulate it. I went over my thoughts until I felt confident to articulate my words, "Babaró, so in essence, you are saying that watching this drama—being in this drama is a gift for me?"

"Oh, yes, without a doubt this is a gift on a grand scale. You are at the level to observe what is occurring and look at it from another perspective. As sometimes people's actions are a hidden message and you must look closer to what is truly happening in their lower level of consciousness."

CHAPTER
SEVEN

I have been in Iowa for ten days now. Babaró told me last weekend that our departure date would be Thursday (yesterday). However that did not happen. Instead, Crystal and I had gone to the hospital to see her father.

Henry had been transferred to another hospital in another city for rehabilitation. As we visited him, there had been multiple interruptions. Our purpose was to give him a healing treatment and talk to him about his feelings of guilt concerning the wreck. Henry had felt he had been at fault. Because of his error in judgment Henry felt unworthy to receive healing or forgiveness.

At one point, crystal slipped out of the room to speak with his physical therapist leaving me alone with Henry. At once I felt a power take over. I said to Henry, "I have two spirit guides who are doctors who I have asked to work with you. Please talk to them and ask them to assist you. Their names are Stephanó and Franklin." Then I got a small piece of paper from my purse and wrote the names down for him adding, I have asked them to stay by your side until you are stable and strong." I said nothing else to him about it.

Babaró spoke to me again saying, "Nakala, it is time that we take our leave from Crystal's home."

Often there are times that I am directed to do something and wonder if it is a teaching to feel with my heart. In this particular instance I told Babaró that I didn't want to leave Crystal without any outside help.

Babaró stated with kindness, "Nakala, you are interfering by remaining. Concerning this lesson: There are many people involved. In order for the lesson to reveal itself in entirety you must remove yourself from this home. Friday morning you are to pack up and leave as early as possible."

My heart sank. Part of me was ready to go but another part of me wanted to remain as I felt Crystal may crumble under the pressures of being the caregiver for two very needy people.

Babaró repeated himself, "It is time, Nakala. We told you before you ever left California that you must follow our directives during this time." I nodded my head and knew he was correct."

CHAPTER
EIGHT

After logging in over 2,500 miles on my car, which included a side-trip back home to Kansas to share Christmas with my family, I have had plenty of time to process the teachings that I had been given while I was away.

It was late, almost 10:00 PM, when I had rolled into my garage in Weed, California. During the entire trip the roads were clear except for the very last hour on highway 5 from Redding to Weed, which had been windy and rainy. Thank God the temperature had been above freezing.

What had concerned me the most had been getting back home safely. I had been practicing different affirmations like: I am always safe; I am always traveling in clear conditions; the sky is clear. I felt like for the most part my journey had been successful.

I knew that I had been guided across the country during a very specific window for my safety and for that I am grateful.

* * *

After I got back home, I had been directed to take three full days off from writing; all the while I had kicked and screamed. I wanted to return to my writing schedule. However, Babaró told me that I was to use this time to do things for myself—to nurture myself. He had commanded me, "Take a salt bath complete with soft music and scented candles. Do some needlework. Maybe work in the yard. Most definitely, you are to rest!" The entire time, though, all I could think of was getting back to my love—the writing. I grew restless and depressed.

Nathanal gave me a bit of advice. "Enjoy this time," he had said, "as tomorrow you will be quite busy. The masters are more than ready to channel the books through you. For you there will be no more idle moments for some time."

During the night a shift had taken place. I woke up feeling refreshed and didn't care one bit if I wrote. In fact, I felt like I would rather continue my rest. I was rather perplexed by the change in my outlook—my drive.

However, directly after breakfast, Babaró was after me to give my editor, Carl, a call concerning the book he was working on, *The Sacred Contract.*

As I was chatting with Carl, he said, "Happy Winter Solstice!" I had been so focused on getting home and being in my space once again that I had completely forgotten the Solstice! I told him that I had been a little depressed the day before. Carl's response was, "You are in tune to nature. Yesterday was the shortest day of the year; coupled with the overcast sky and the new moon today…well," he explained, "it is understandable that you felt that way."

With that information a new light was shed on why I was directed to get home, when I had, and why I had been guided to rest for the last three days.

"Nakala," Babaró said, "it would be most helpful if you would chart the moon phases and abide by the energy of that time. Having a physical body coupled with an emotional body you are in rhythm with the earth and the moon cycles, not only, but the variances of the astrological alignments. Specific emotions are heightened at certain times simply due to the rhythm of the tides which is controlled by the moon. It is all due to the magnetic gravitational pulls. Your body feels it all!

"A new moon marks new beginnings. We felt in order to benefit all for the highest good we would wait until today to begin anew."

Amazed, I saw yet another facet of Babaró's teaching. I am in awe by how the guides got me home safely and so quickly *and* in enough time for me to rest before getting back to my writing.

All the while, my travel home was in complete alignment with the teaching back in Iowa where I was to support Crystal as she had gone through a critical phase in her life. I was to step back in certain areas so the family members would step up and take responsibility. This had all been coordinated with the weather patterns *and* the moon phases!

In addition, I was able stop in Kansas to spend quality time with each of *my* family members for Christmas. I am sure there are more reasons that I was to have this experience. They just haven't come to light as of yet.

I felt Babaró's energy and sensed he was ready to take over with the writing. It was as if Babaró was telepathically telling me (without words) his ideas for the book as a flood of subjects came to the surface of my mind in one instant. As quickly as they had surfaced they vanished.

"Yes, I am ready to commence with the teachings." Babaró affirmed.

"Nakala, from the moment you were called to go to Iowa almost a month has passed and with it you have gained a host of opportunities for growth. What a rare and treasured gift you have received. The thing is, Nakala, you are still gleaning from the experience and as you go forward in your days to come, more of the lesson will be brought to the surface and integrated into particular levels of your consciousness. You listened to your heart and went across the nation and because of this you will never be the same.

"During this lesson you have faced one of your fears: the fear of traveling alone over long distances. No more will you travel alone, in fear, as you have faced this fear over and over again. You have become accustomed to facing the unknown in peace.

"The world is like a gigantic stage—all of you being actors playing your part to learn particular lessons. I tell you plainly: when you do not learn a particular lesson in fullness you are given again the same lesson. Usually the lesson is given in a different setting with different players. You must pay heed to all or you may find yourself in places—in situations that may be rather painful. Your Higher Self *will* get your attention, Miss, know it!

"We are pleased, Nakala that you listened to your higher guidance. You saw the wisdom in several of the directives that you were given. Thank you for making this teaching a joyful experience for us all."

I questioned Babaró's choice of words…*joyful? Seriously?* I knew there had been times (many) when I had questioned what I was hearing and told them outright that I couldn't—wouldn't do something. Like the day I was directed to leave Iowa and Crystal had been a mess. Henry hadn't even come home from the hospital yet. Because of Crystal's and my unique relationship, I had been able to openly speak to her about Babaró's directive to pack up and leave. Yet, I told her I would wait a bit longer. She had been weighing her options of how to care for her parents. We all knew it was time to hire some outside help. Now, it was a matter of Crystal sitting down and making phone calls to find someone.

I had waited another day until Crystal's father had been released from the hospital before I packed to go. Even then I had questioned my guidance.

"Nakala," Babaró interrupted my thoughts, "Listen, to have a student who listens and follows *is* for us a joyful experience. No, not every moment on that journey was met with perfection—some moments were met with resistance but in the end you did exactly as you should have by consciously following not only our guidance but your heart's guidance. We are quite pleased. We had set before you a time for all to come together—for all to fall into place like a well-tailored dinner jacket. The jacket was to fit snuggly—comfortably without restricting movement in any area. I speak of Crystal's brothers stepping in to assist the family, Henry's discharge from the hospital, the weather conditions, and the alignment of the solar orbit. In addition, all was in placement to share Christmas with your own family—their availability. Yes, there were many other lessons given during this time. All is to come to the surface as the writings proceed.

"I'd like to share with you one other bit of information that you may find helpful while you process the teachings. Crystal's family witnessed a great sacrifice made by you. You drove across the country in the dead of winter in order to assist the family. Crystal's brothers saw this gift and were able to use it to shift their stubborn nature and open up to giving forth their time in a more generous fashion. I speak of loving and giving forth assistance not only when it is warranted but simply because it *feels* good to do so! I speak of *love.*

"In essence, much of the resentment was dismantled—let go of. Crystal's brothers had been wrestling with thoughts of giving up their free time to care for aging parents verses how much easier it would be to place them in a nursing facility. You see? Oft times it takes one person to show the way. When you packed your things and left the state you had absolutely no idea what you were truly doing. All you knew was how you felt—what your heart told you and that it was time to go."

* * *

"Nakala you are quite aware that we will use any opportunity to teach you what may come along. Your drive home from Iowa was no exception. Even though we proficiently guided you through the many states, we were constantly using different situations/tools to teach you. The weather was merely one.

"Throughout your travels and the stays at the various motels you had moments to meditate, read, and listen to the radio and so on. All were opportunities to learn to listen to your heart and your logical mind without going into fear. You were given snippets of information to bring forth thought, emotion, and action.

"Which brings me to this: One evening during your stay at a hotel you were reading the *Autobiography of a Yogi*. Yogananda, the author, had explained that his master/guru had gifted him with his name, Paramahansa Yogananda. This information took you promptly back to the time that you had been instructed to legally take the name Nakala Maria Angelic Akasie. You were gifted with this name shortly after you had begun to channel our messages and be it known, was of no coincidence, was also given to you during the process of publication of your first book, *When Angels Speak: The Awakening: A Pleiadian Endeavor.*

"However, in your mind, you thought it was a huge hick-up that you had already had your book printed displaying your married name Jackie Mullinax and now you were being Divinely directed to change your name legally. You asked us, 'How on earth would your followers find you now?'

"As a new author the marketing was difficult enough but now you had the incorrect name printed on dozens of hard copies of the book.

You were unable to see your way through this ordeal. We told you all was in order and to understand that *we* knew what we were doing as we always do.

"After your initial shock of having this new found ability to channel Beings of Light, you found yourself feeling somewhat vulnerable. Nevertheless, there inside you lay a tiny seed that had been fertilized. The seed had been nurtured somewhat and was preparing to birth a great Divine power that of which you had never known before. (I speak of steps you have taken during this embodiment.) You had an undeniable realization of your true purpose as you had attained a heightened awareness; an invincible knowing that you *had* to do this *thing*, which was to actively participate and record all transmissions from not only your guides but the countless others who traveled the galactic highways and to also post many of the messages in your blogs and books!

"The main message given was there are many about who are assisting not only the planet Earth but the peoples (all life forms and intelligences) that reside therein. That these beings are here to assist for the highest good! You questioned, how would your followers find this instrumental message if you changed your name mid-stream?

"In retrospect, the seemingly insignificant paragraph that Yogananda wrote had refueled a memory that required a convincing explanation in order for you to not only fully comprehend, but to appreciate enabling you to go forward with the gift of your spiritual name.

"I give to the reader some background information. Nakala was born as Jacquelyn Jolene Black in 1958, although you went by the name Jackie Black until 1975, when you married taking on a different name— your married name, Jackie Mullinax. Each name change reflects a new segment or chapter of your sojourn on the Earth plane. This is common: to take on a different name when there is a significant transition in one's life.

"When you spiritually awakened to the prospect of having a real and intentional relationship with your Pleiadian family to follow your *true* chosen path of service, again, your name was changed reflecting this transformation to Nakala Maria Angelic Akasie."

"Yes," I agreed, "I remember Father Quem coming and telling me to change my name and to make it legal. I had done so, but not without a gut-wrenching fear of being rejected and labeled (as crazy) by my peers, my family.

"However, I was able to move through it gracefully and complete the task. Just the other day, a friend was talking to me—referring to something I had done in the past. This friend had been using my old name, Jackie. (This person still hadn't shifted to accept my new name.) I truly didn't know who my friend had been referring to. I asked, 'Jackie? Who are you talking about?' I knew then that I had integrated my name, Nakala, fully."

"Nakala, may I remind you that you overcame the feelings of fear connected to your name change? The adversity you encountered as you plodded forward took much courage. All were pleased that you faced this task, never giving up."

I wondered to myself if someone in the family, like in the Native American cultures, decides what name is given to someone and asked, "Babaró what I want to know is who picked my name and why that particular name was chosen?"

As soon as I had typed my question a power overtook me literally shaking me. My heart expanded and then I heard the words, "I speak!" Immediately I knew that Father Quem would be gifting me with the answers I so desired. To be honest I felt a little anxious. His energy was intense and my body responded. It was almost as if I had a huge weight sitting on my chest. I found it difficult to breathe. I decided then that I should move away from my desk for a few minutes, sit in my recliner and mediate while I did some deep breathing.

For the last fifteen minutes I had known that it was time to get up from my chair. Yet, I had put it off. Why had my choice been to take a few moments to myself at that precise time?

As I assessed my motivation behind my action, I suspected that I had implemented a tactic of sorts, a diversion maybe. I did my meditation and found I was more relaxed. Then I moved into the kitchen and made a cup of tea and did some stretches before I returned to my desk. Still my chest hurt and I wanted to just cry. I love my father, Quem, and am so grateful for his guidance. However, today his energy was intense and uncomfortable for me. I wasn't sure I wanted to hear the story about my name. I didn't want to cry.

"Nakala, dearest," Quem began without a single hint of impatience, "there are days, many, that I am in wait for certain questions to be asked by you! At last I am given this opportunity to share the reasons behind your name change. Ah…'Nakala'…such a beautiful song, is it not?" Quem paused for many moments waiting for me to answer. I sat retrieving memories of the times I had given out my name, Nakala. Be it to a person or even a group and how many times they had complemented me on it, saying, "How beautiful it sounds." Always they commented that they had never heard the name before. But never had I associated my name with a song. But yes, it did sound like a song or a soft spring breeze perhaps.

"Nakala," Quem resumed, "just as I was gifted long ago with the pleasure of naming you, Cathryn, after your birth into our family on Pleiades so was I gifted with naming you Nakala Maria Angelic Akasie after your last transition. In a sense, you had been reborn. The rebirthing had been a difficult process in some respects but I tell you adversity makes strong! I personally selected your name, Nakala. I chose the name that would produce the tones that suit you and also assist you in the future for the highest benefit."

Having done years of genealogy research and seen how we take on family names I was interested in knowing how Pleiadian's picked names I asked, "Father, did you name me after someone?"

"No, my daughter," Quem answered with sincerity, "there is naught a single soul that I look unto or revere in as much that I would choose to name you after. You were to keep the Akasie name, of course, to testify your connection with us. Your name is quite original and was given to you to signify—remind you of your quest on earth during this time. Your name means to surrender oneself in service to God. Your name serves as a reminder, to you, of who you are and your grand purpose— your chosen path during this life-stream.

"I might add that when Nathanal whispers your name in your ear the sound is quite beautiful. Your name was carefully selected, be it known.

The name is soft like a caress. One cannot speak your name without receiving love on some level." I thought he was finished and secretly hoped that he was. Emotionally, I was overwrought—spent. Receiving the answers to the questions that had remained in my sub-conscious mind for so long wasn't so easy, especially from my father.

But he hadn't been complete with his say. Quem began again, "I just gave you a short time to gather yourself," Quem explained. "You have calmed yourself somewhat. I aim to make my mark in fullness. Names are words. They all have tone—color—vibration. These tones are encoded constantly, aligning, balancing, and reawakening or reactivating your Divine Cosmic Being which in itself is encoded. The tones serve as a communicator to remind, so to speak, to keep alive—to *remember*! The name, Nakala, as well, assists in taking you to the next level of evolution—your ascension, constantly aligning and unifying your energetic bodies that make you whole and complete. Truly, your name is a sweet song—a breath of fresh air—a declaration—an everlasting tribute to God, our Creator, of your surrender in service to Him.

"Remember this teaching given from this day forth, as you hear, not only, but as you *feel* your name spoken by others or yourself, it is like a tender embrace to soften, to love. Your name is energy as you are. Your name is a gift—a sweet melody, as you are, my dearest, Nakala. Your name is meant to serve to beautify all in its path, as you are. Energy travels, my Dearest, and joins with like energy. Every time your name is thought on or spoken, energy is created—beautiful it is. I say this: every time someone thinks on you, how is it they remember you? Your love? Your compassion? Your willingness to serve? I am your Father. I love you beyond measure. Every thought, emotion, and action created by you is to be set with the purpose to serve Father-Mother-God to the best of your ability. Because you serve God you serve the PEOPLE. *I AM QUEM.*"

PART
FOUR

MASTER TULRÓ

Being a new resident in the Mt. Shasta area, I am still learning the best places to shop, trying out different events to meet people (to find where I fit in), and ultimately where I may serve. The books continue to be written and I feel so blessed to be surrounded by a host of angels, masters, and guides. I am aware that the devas, elementals, faeries, and sprites are in wait for me to begin communications with them and know this is part of the *why* I have come to live in the mountains of northern California. Being in nature will help restore me, heal me, and ultimately bring me into balance.

All of a sudden, I heard someone speak with a heavy accent—an accent that I could not identify or connect to a particular country or culture. But the way the words were pronounced sounded a little like the way the Pleiadian Ascended Master Tulró speaks.

Then the words shifted to another language—one I have heard—channeled many times in the past but don't understand. Repeatedly, I heard the word(s), "A-towie-ana" (phonetic spelling). Truly I had no idea what it means.

Politely, I asked, "Who is speaking to me?" I heard the same being say, "Tulró."

A sense of happiness sored through me as I exclaimed, "Oh, it is you. I kind of wondered if it might be you but I haven't talked to you in such a long time, I wasn't sure."

Enthusiastically, Tulró repeated his message but this time was kind enough to translate it for me. "I say to you a-towie-ana. I work! I bring!" Obviously, Tulró was excited about something.

"We have decided, Babaró and I, to shake things up a bit." In my inner eye, I saw Tulró shake his head in an overly exuberant manner. Well, I thought, if anyone can liven things up around here it is Tulró. The last I had heard anything about Tulró he was working with Crystal at her home. Tulró is known for stirring the pot a bit. He has worked in the contrary with me by tempting or testing me with things that are not for my highest good. Over time I have learned that I do not have to follow the pack to be accepted. I can say no! I wondered if he were here to test me again.

"Miss," Tulró began, "You are always being tested, know it! Because of the state affairs—the peoples of your world have sunken down to the level of listening to an imaginary being—their ego—for direction. Now, Nakala, you are being trained, if you will, to listen to your heart, your inner guidance. You are accepting this guidance on a conscious level.

"Do you remember when I used to taunt you with cappuccinos?" In my inner mind I saw Tulró wink, heard him laugh, and then slap his knee. Nice, I thought. Oh boy, do I remember. The sweet creamy drinks were, at the time, to me, a slice of heaven. No more though, as my life, my world, has changed dramatically in that department.

"Yes," I heard Tulró say, "no more will you succumb to my influences—the likes of cappuccinos or other foodstuffs that are sugary." Intuitively, I knew why Tulró had come to speak. I felt a tightness in my stomach as anxiety began to build. The topic Tulró wanted to discuss is a sensitive issue, and for me, seemed a bit private: my diet and what had happened to change it.

Boldly, I heard myself ask, "Is this really necessary? Aren't there other subjects that would benefit our audience just as much or even more?" I saw him shake his head, no, as he answered, "Perhaps."

The way Tulró acts reminds me of a leprechaun, in fact he *looks* like a leprechaun with his dark curly hair and pointed chin! On many occasions, I have seen his mischievous grin and a twinkle in his eye as he has prodded me. Countless times I have seen him *work* me.

When he began to *mentor* Crystal I saw it all again—his tactics—his style. I had to laugh. Crystal knew all about Tulró's antics as I had shared several "Tulró" stories with her. When he had showed up at her house it was I who was full of joy. No more would I be aggravated by Tulró and his silly pranks. Crystal and I, both, knew how Tulró charmed his students—what his *expertise* was.

Tulró is full of joy no matter what the situation is and seems to take immense pleasure in his teaching. Inwardly, I chuckled as I revisited memories of him taunting me with different foods [and men]. The *and men* was Tulró's little addition—his way of making a joke.

All of a sudden, I was struck with the realization that I had been played by Tulró once again as of late I had witnessed a buildup of conversations concerning an old flame, Allen. But it had been Nathanal who had mentioned Allen. Little by little Nathanal has eased Allen into our conversation; saying how it would be good if I just picked up the phone to call him.

Just last evening, I laid in bed ready to surrender to sweet dreams, when Nathanal began to speak to me in a manner that I recognized instantly. In a very subtle style, Nathanal was shrewdly working to convince me to call Allen. Allen was back in Kansas and I had not spoken to him since I had arrived in California.

Nathanal had gone on about how nice it would be to reconnect with Allen—to see how he was faring—to wish him a Merry Christmas. Purposely, I had waited until this morning to decide.

Although, I had absolutely no desire to directly speak to Allen, it did seem like a nice gesture. Nathanal had been speaking to me about just *checking in* to see how he was doing. "It would be so nice to let him know you are thinking of him. What would it hurt?" Nathanal had asked me like he had genuinely cared about me doing this thing—genuinely care about Allen. I saw *test* written all over it. Nathanal had used all his cards to persuade—entice—convince me until I had felt that little tug in my heart or so I had thought. So I finally resigned and picked up my phone and punched in his number.

"Miss Nakala," Tulró began, "it is time you learn what is guiding you forward. Is it compassion, sympathy, love, guilt, or someone else altogether?"

"Look Tulró, this is a great lesson, I give you that, but I honestly did not and do not want to speak to this man and luckily he didn't pick up. The only reason I called him was because of *someone else's* insistence."

I felt put-off and even a little angry that Tulró had joined forces with Nathanal to coax me into doing something that was not for my highest good. For days, Nathanal had made little remarks working me… prodding me. For me there was no question, I have absolutely no desire to contact him and I had stayed the course…for a while until dear Nathanal had succeeded in wearing me down and today I had simply caved to get him off my back.

"Nakala, you must know what is for your highest good always. You must not allow another to persuade you into something that you *feel* would not benefit you.

"Take food for instance…how many times did I put before you the idea of buying a cappuccino? Every time the word was mentioned your memory kicked in of how delicious the drink smelled and tasted—how it made you feel; even if it was only a temporary lift. Never mind the fact that it was laced with chemicals that were harmful, even addictive.

"Now, you easily recognize that you have had the propensity to be lured into certain situations and kept there by feelings of guilt, not only, but with feelings that you must assist in certain ways just because you arrived on the scene when it *seemed* that the person just couldn't manage on their own. Nakala, I give to you this: There are certain lessons that people, themselves, must go through in order to learn. You are to ask always before you assist another. Perhaps it isn't for you to get involved."

"Oh, wait a minute, Tulró you are changing the subject here."

"Yes!" he said with determination and conviction, "I take you back to the Iowa trip to assist Crystal. You went because of your love for Crystal and her family. You knew she was in a bind. You were available to support her for a time. She required a person to be a sounding board and to assist with the household chores. Unbeknownst to you or her, for that matter, you were there to act as a role model; to show other family members that if an outsider can freely give their time perhaps they can as well. Your presence served in this capacity. When we saw Crystal's brothers shift in attitude—thought and emotion we directed you to leave Iowa. You were to disengage your energy by leaving the property in order for others to fulfill their own contracts."

Attentively, I had been listening to Tulro give me the detailed reasons behind some of the directives I had been given, but still wanted some clarity. "Tulró, so you are saying that you used the cappuccinos as a tool or primary lesson for me and later built upon that? My ego wanted satisfaction so I had just gone and bought one. Basically, I could have easily become a slave in that regard—always feeding my ego through my physical desires."

"Nakala, you *were* a slave in the respect that each time I mentioned Cappuccinos you wanted one. Every time I waved the cappuccino napkin at you whether you were on the road or not, 'Hey, Nakala do you want to get a cappuccino?' You received the word—the stimuli—the code to trigger the desire to partake. And partake you did!

"The cappuccino tasted good and temporarily it made you feel good. But it was all short-lived, Nakala, only lasting for a few short minutes. You knew that these drinks did not benefit you physically but emotionally it had served as a comfort: a fix. The drink soothed you, calmed you, and on a particular level it made you feel loved by yourself. You bought the drink did you not? You gave it to yourself. It was a nice gesture and you enjoyed it. For you, this was a way to show yourself that you were worthy to receive: to love yourself. During the teaching you had not built a strong foundation concerning the concept of loving yourself. Love does not come from material sources. Love comes from within oneself: the heart.

"True love for yourself is to take proper care of your bodies all—standing up to the enticements or persuasions of others or even yourself and saying with sincerity, 'No thank you. I do appreciate your offer, but at this time I do not wish to partake.'

"You have received this lesson may times over. You knew that I was testing you with the cappuccinos. Subconsciously, I was asking, you over and over, Nakala, 'Are you strong enough to love yourself on this level by saying no?' It wasn't until you became ill and was forced to change your diet that you really looked at what you put in your body.

"Nakala, this teaching is multifaceted and also for the collective. The collective consciousness has, right before their very own eyes and even with their very own knowing, I might add, been allowing themselves to be held hostage by the lure of advertising to buy the fast food commodities—coffees are just one of the products I speak of.

"Most everything available that is mass produced is laced with corn syrup or sugar. Sugar is addictive leaving you wanting for more. It is a vicious cycle that many people are entrenched in. Sooner or later the physical body will no longer tolerate the products as they will be unable to digest or flush the system of chemicals that are not meant for human consumption.

"The human body is like a mechanical device. Would you fuel your car with something different than petrol—other than what was intended for it? It simply wouldn't work; the cogs would bind immediately. The human body, because of its great ability to adapt, may continue on for some time, but not for forever. You have seen the rise in disease: diabetes, cancers, arthritis, and the basic degeneration of the human body.

"The problem herein lies in the food industry." Tulró had stopped his teaching waiting for me to assess his last statement before he continued on, "Or does it? In order to generate a larger profit, businesses often times do what is necessary to keep expenses as low as possible. In the food industry, this means to put in fillers like starches and/or to artificially enhance their products by adding sugars and/or other foodstuffs that not only keep cost down but ensure higher sales and profits because these additives are addictive in nature; not necessarily being nutritious. It fulfills a *desire* like the cappuccinos. You see? And it keeps the customers coming back."

I thought about what Tulró had said and was in total agreement. As a marketing strategy, some businesses have enticed customers to purchase products even if it is not something that is for their highest good. We must use discernment.

Tulró allowed me to further examine his message before he proceeded. "But it goes further. The food industry is complying with the consumers' lifestyles. People are in a time-crunch. Because of the demands of the material world (all self-imposed, mind you) people simply do not prioritize the importance of nutrition and many are not even conscious of what they are putting into their bodies, what their bodies require to be healthy, or how not eating properly compromises the body.

"Once consumers catch on realizing the importance of healthy diets they will begin to buy healthier foods. In turn, the food industry will offer foods that will reflect the demands of the consumer."

I saw the catch and asked, "Who is going to change first?"

Tulró's response was, 'When people get so sick from their food, I dare say, it will be them who demand a change. You, Nakala, have experienced it firsthand. In order to live in a body free of pain you had to change your diet. Did you not?"

There had been no question to the truth of what Tulró said. "You are correct. In order for me to be pain free I had to make some drastic changes. But first, I had to learn to love myself enough to make the changes.

"Tulró, I would like to talk a bit on what I have experienced first. I believe that when people are open to what the causes and effects are, people will learn faster.

"In order to change my diet I saw that my digestive tract was slow and as time went on was becoming more blocked. The funny thing about this is it took me literally years for me to question if there was anything really wrong. I did not know what normal was. As a child growing up there were two things that were taboo in conversation: toilet and sexual habits."

"Constipation, hemorrhoids, weight issues were some of the main symptoms that I had been dealing with. These symptoms were caused by an underlying root. As a society we eat vast amounts of wheat (gluten) and other refined starches that for me are not easily digested. Instead, what was happening in my intestines was something far from normal. The gluten was acting like *glue* and staying in my intestines far longer than anything is supposed to stay there. In other words, it just sat there blocking the system. My body tried to adapt, work to free the build-up in my intestines by creating pockets or crevices and polyps.

"My body was swimming in toxic matter. Nice image, but maybe this will get through to the readers. All of this snowballed. My intestines were damaged. My entire system had been compromised. I was not able, through the small intestines (the villi), to uptake the proper nutrition any longer from the food rich in nutrition that I did consume. This caused a slow decline in the flora in my bowels causing an imbalance. The good bacteria had been declining as the bad bacteria rose. The longer I neglected the issue the worse it became.

"It wasn't long when I noticed that any breads or starches caused problems. I am talking about candida which had gone systemic. In order to correct the issue I had to stop ingesting gluten. Because of the overgrowth in bad bacteria I began to see symptoms. I had created a toxic environment which sugar fed. As I began to research my symptoms I saw that sugar or corn syrup was in almost everything I ate and drank. The cappuccinos were one of the very first things taken off my diet.

"Slowly I have exchanged fresh vegetables for bread and different canned or prepackaged foods. I have really had to open my eyes and carefully read labels on all canned and prepackaged foods. The foods that are mass produced (even the items you think are safe) are often filled with things to enhance the taste and are often unbeneficial.

"I am not a doctor. I have not studied in depth the working of the human body. However, I have witnessed first-hand what the common American diet has done to me. Slowly, with the assistance of two of my guides, who are medical doctors and surgeons, coupled with Ascended Masters, like Tulró, I am on the road to recovery."

CHAPTER
TEN

It has been a year since I first received that message to leave Kansas City. It hardly seems possible that so much time has passed. I have found myself well-established and happy in a place half-way across the nation! Just then I was shown the letter L and a little voice whispered, "Leave." What? Then I was directed to look at a little mirror and that same small voice said, "*Hold the vision.*"

I had just been tested. The question was: would I fall into guilt as I revisited leaving family and friends behind like I had abandoned them or would I *hold the vision* of what my heart desires?

A really close friend of mine from Kansas, Cathy had called, interrupting me from getting started with writing. She had been my neighbor for several years. Having been raised in the South she embraces old fashioned values. One being men are to look after their women.

Immediately I recognized that Cathy had been drinking enough to have a more than noticeable effect on her speech. Her words were slurred and she was repeating them in that fanciful way drunks often do. Cathy had begun to drink heavily after her last car wreck. (She had been involved in two really devastating wrecks that had occurred within two years of each other.) Dozens of broken bones and many surgeries and months of therapy later, I saw a dramatic shift take place in Cathy. I have tried to look the other way. But honestly, I feel, in order to remain connected with her, something must change. I no longer feel like I can look the other direction—pretend everything is okay—pretend it is okay for her to call me when she is drunk. No longer am I willing to sit and listen to her incessant ramblings.

Point blank, Cathy had asked me several personal questions. The first didn't surprise me as Cathy had been with me during my divorce. She wanted to see me with a man who would care for me. Cathy had asked if I had found that hunka hunka (man of my dreams). I had to admit that no, I hadn't. Then she asked me if I were happy, truly happy. I had to say that yes, I am happy as I am doing exactly what I want to do and in the place I want to do it! But my friend persisted and told me how she loved me and missed me, then she began to sob uncontrollably. Even so, after what I presumed to be a dramatic attempt to get me to feel sorry for her and feel guilty for my decision, I do not want to return to Kansas now or in the near future. I have found my spot and for now I am going to stay here.

Suddenly, the energy in the room shifted and I knew Samuel Paul was getting ready to get on with his teaching and take over with the writing. He had said he wanted to give me a message and for me to relax. Receiving the phone call had upset me somewhat so he had waited.

I love Cathy and am so sorry that she is going through this. My friend needs help. The kind of help she requires I cannot give.

"Nakala," Samuel Paul began, "The teachings were postponed a bit. We knew the call from Cathy was coming through so we waited."

"Many times people turn to the drink in an effort to cope with issues and pain. Cathy suffers from not only physical pain, but grief and a deep agony—a fatigue that never seems to let up. She is exhausted from being imprisoned in a physical body that no longer serves her for the highest good. We desire greatly to see her heal. But for now it is her lesson. She is to listen to her angels—her heart. One day, we pray soon, she will seek what she requires for true healing."

"Samuel Paul, I honestly don't know if you will talk on this subject but Cathy has gone through so many *accidents* since I have known her. I would certainly appreciate if you would guide me with your wisdom on the matter. These two car wrecks nearly killed her. Within a year of the last car wreck she had a kidney removed and then fell off her porch and broke her shoulder. This happened before I left Kansas. Since then her kitchen caught fire and God knows what else she has been through. I have known her for over fifteen years and during that time her house has continually leaked water incurring major water damage. The thing is, she is more educated when it comes to energy and has always taken great care of herself and her property. Cathy loves people!"

"Nakala," Samuel Paul said, "you were Divinely guided to leave Kansas for many reasons." Instantly, I sensed where he was going with his statement. But, instead he veered entirely away from his statement in another direction.

"Constantly, people are creating energy—having experiences derived from said energy. Cathy is no exception. We give a little background here. You met Cathy when your children were in their younger years. The two families had similar situations concerning challenges with the children. Cathy and you grew to be close friends, not just because of the issues with the children but because your energy resonated. During that time your personalities were energetically compatible.

"Also, there is karma to tend with. Many of the people are still working on karmic issues and until they learn about the Sacred Fire and the dispensations the Karmic Board has granted they will continue to do so for a while longer—what we perceive as the hard way - through old fashioned works.

"Your friend has had a karmic issue she is paying on. In addition, there are issues now, during this life that she has not dealt with in entirety compounding the process. Without going into detail, I'll say this: she continues to work on particular lessons and as she is plodding through them she creates her reality with her own thoughts, emotions, and actions.

"Collisions with anything (vehicles in this case) indicate a conflict in your thoughts, emotions, and actions. In other words she is in inner turmoil—that hasn't been fully dealt with properly or at all. There are choices that have been offered up but the choice taken was either not made or incorrect to be in alignment with the Higher Self.

"In this case (the car collisions) were given as an extreme wake-up call to assess all aspects of one's life and make the necessary adjustments bringing back into alignment. In other words, the life path had become so skewed that in the physical reality it has manifested as a collision. The collision is a manifestation of the choices to stop, go left, or right, and so on. In other words, it is a time to get clear on what direction you are to take. Unfortunately, the assessment wasn't taken before the collision. Because there was a physical hit—damage to the body there has been ample time to reflect, change direction and to heal."

"Wait!" I said, "Cathy wasn't even driving. Her husband was!" "Ah, but Cathy was in the vehicle. It was for her, as well as her husband, to assess. The two of them, the husband and wife, are in direct conflict concerning several issues—issues that continue to be overshadowed or ignored outright. The energy continues to grow."

Samuel Paul was on a roll not pausing before he asked, "The fall from the porch? Where did Cathy land?" I answered, "On the ground, Samuel Paul, and she hit a three and a half foot decorative steel angel on her way down."

"Yes, umm. This is a very symbolic incident. I'd say this is a directive telling her to get grounded. You can't get much clearer on that one.

"I go on." Samuel Paul said, "The energies that are being created in that family continue to grow and are escalating out of control. The drink is all a way to suppress—keep at bay what she is truly thinking and feeling but not communicating."

Suddenly, Samuel Paul stopped his dictation and directed me to look at the letter E for energy and then to an O but I was directed to look inside the O. This meant to reconnect with my Higher Self and fill up the void I had made with Light and Love. His specific message that may be viewed as cryptic was presented to make me think—to go back just a bit and see how my thoughts had become conflicted. The message, like a surreal dream that begged to be interpreted, had been there all along concerning Cathy. However, I had not stopped to ask for guidance on what I may do to assist. At this point, I questioned if there was anything I could do for her or her family.

"Nakala, now, I speak of why you were guided to leave Kansas. As it was in Iowa, it was in Kansas. The teachings were multifaceted—multilayered. One reason you were guided to leave the area away from family and friends as these people have lessons they are to go through. One of those lessons is to learn to gracefully let go of people allowing them to go forth on their journey freely. You are a traveler and there are times many when you are called to go and this is to be done without judgment from *anyone!*"

CHAPTER
ELEVEN

My guides were prompting me, yet again, to get back into Yoga. They went so far as to set a schedule for me to incorporate this discipline into my weekly routine. I was a little surprised because Nathanal had specifically told me, "Rearrange your schedule." I had openly argued with him saying that I liked my schedule the way it was. Well, I did!

Nathanal kindly reminded me that I was to stay flexible and that meant if it took rearranging my work schedule to get me back into the practice of Yoga then so be it!

Understanding the importance of an exercise regimen and how it assists in so many ways to balance the mind, body, and spirit I had agreed to try a change in my schedule since it would be best.

Because of the shift, I suddenly found myself having a day off from writing that I didn't expect. It was time to get groceries so I headed for Mt. Shasta City and did my shopping. I thought this would be all the errands I'd do for the day and I'd head home and read or work on the beading I had started for a Native American smudge feather handle.

Instead, though, after I got home and put away my groceries, I was directed to get in the car again and drive to another city to look for some herbs to assist me with a cleanse I wanted to begin.

The area I live in is well protected by trees. I call it my enchanted forest and it is like living in my own individual bubble. I love it here but to see the open sky is just not possible. I do have a nice view of Mt. Shastina and Mt. Shasta though.

As I was driving out of my bubble, I noticed a lenticular cloud that was near Mt. Shasta. I am fascinated by these clouds, knowing instinctively that they are space ships in disguise.

Little by little the beings from other planets and star systems are allowing us to become familiar with the fact that they are here, watching, waiting, and assisting us whenever and wherever they are allowed. All is monitored by the Galactic Federation and different Councils of Light ensuring that all is in Divine order.

Being enamored by the sight, I found a place to turn my car around and take some pictures before I traveled on. It is common but a bit on the perplexing side to see these clouds hang in the same location for a few days before disappearing into the ethers.

Two hours later, after I had completed my shopping in three stores, I headed back home and immediately saw the cloud still there suspended in the very same location and sustaining the exact same shape as before.

Call me sentimental if you will, but when I see these *clouds* I am bathed in this energy and easily overcome with gratitude and love. This time had been no exception.

As I watched the cloud formation I was gushing on to Nathanal about how spectacular the site was when I saw another cloud begin to gather energy and take shape directly under the lenticular cloud. Quickly it grew to its allotted size and finished its detail. I wondered what was happening before me. I continued to watch the cloud until the form was complete. It was a figure of a woman lying on her back directly under the craft and she was holding a baby. The details were plain to see: her face, her hair, her bosom, dress…even her feet and then the swaddled babe that she held in her arms. The message was: you are always cared for, always protected.

Needless to say, my emotion was getting the best of me. I was stunned and tears began to form and spill over.

I was literally lifted from my third/forth dimensional reality no longer aware of the fact that I was driving my car down the busy freeway. Some would call me ungrounded.

At once my mind began to formulate questions in regard to who the spacecraft belonged to. I really wasn't expecting an answer so quickly. Noticeably, Nathanal had become excited but simultaneously his voice had thickened-deepened with feelings of gratitude and respect as he answered, "It is ours. It is from the Pleiades."

Nathanal, without prompting disclosed the name of the ship, *El Don Quin.* Without thinking I quickly reached for my purse and found a scrap of note paper to write the name down just as Nathanal, began to speak on the ship to explain its function. "The lenticular cloud or spaceship is stationed in a particular area for the purpose of transporting goods and people to or from Telos (to the star people who live in the city inside of Mt. Shasta), not only, but the ship is like a small city with a landing post that smaller ships use as a home base. The ship is used as a post for trade with other ships of the Pleiadian nation as well as other nations. Nathanal concluded it was not used for squadrons or as a command post for the academy or military but for transports."

As if reading my mind, Nathanal said, "No, Mother and Father are not staying on this ship." (Nathanal was referring to Quem and Sarah our Pleiadian parents.)

As soon as I got home and had put away my purchases, I retrieved the small piece of paper from my purse and reread what I had scribbled down: *El Don Quin.* Directly, I went to my computer and logged on to the Internet and did a search on the name. I knew El, in Spanish meant, *The.* As I went further in my search I remembered The Ascended Master El Morya. El, I had learned meant, *of God.* Not knowing the Pleiadian language I began to see similarities in this name with Spanish and then Portuguese. I looked at some of the names of my guides, Tulró, Stephanó, Telmure, Babaró… They could be considered to have a Spanish influence. Maybe it was the Spaniards who had a Pleiadian influence. I kept searching. For me this was like a game. All along, I had been given bits of information or clues to build from. They had served to stimulate my mind and inherently make learning about the star nations enjoyable!

I continued to play around with the sequence of words. Until finally I concluded that the name of the ship must be something like, *The Wise One, The Intelligent One, The Wise and or Intelligent Gift of God.*

After I went as far as I could with the interpretation, I asked Nathanal if I had gotten it correct. His response was, "There are many translations, but the one I give to you is, *The Gift of God.* You see, El is Of God. Don in Spanish denotes wisdom or an elder or Gift. Quin denotes wisdom intelligence or Counsel."

As I searched on the Internet I found it to be interesting how each language basically meant the same thing but used variations of the same words.

The day after I had seen the beautiful cloud, I had relayed the story to a few people, my biological mother included. She is in her late eighties and continues to be rich in mind. My mother said, "You know I think I have heard of that name before."

I had the same feeling.

PART
FIVE

LETMAR
FROM THE STAR OF KETMIRH

CHAPTER
TWELVE

The next day I was directed to get organized—go through several large loose binders and discard different outdated material and file new printouts that I had acquired lately. I took it as a prompting for a new beginning and to get my act together not realizing that the activity was multifaceted—as usual.

As I was working on the project, I ran across several typed pages of channeled transmissions from a man from *outer space*. He had identified his self to me as Letmar. The contact had been initiated in January of 2011. He had seemed rather enthralled with our communications, so when the transmissions had ended rather abruptly I had wondered why.

The first thing I learned about this fellow, Letmar, was he was adamant how I pronounced his name. It sounded like Lamur and it was meant to sound like the word rolled off the tongue. I recognized the similarity in pronunciation of his name and the word Lemuria and reminded of the sunken continent of Lemuria and the Lemurians who have taken residence inside Mount Shasta in Northern California. However, I had never been given any indication that there was any sort of link between the two names.

Distinctly, in the beginning of the communications, I remembered being thrilled to have this connection but as the transmissions continued forward I had fallen into suspicion, doubt, and then ultimately fear as he had asked me to do something that I was not comfortable in talking about and definitely not comfortable in doing.

Note to the reader: You will notice that in Letmar's transmission he didn't speak fluent English. I inserted words to ease the flow of his transmissions.

This is the second transmission. The first was either lost or not recorded.

LETMAR TRANSMISSION

Yes, I come to you! You wonder as I told you I would come to give you the words you so desire this week. You found yourself inundated with other works and thought the week had passed without our joining.

I hear you wanting your tea. Please go and fulfill that desire. I wait for you to come to me.

Thank you, Letmar. You know I was just getting ready for you. I guess you were aware that I was creating a new file folder here on my computer to store your transmissions. There was not even a short pause. As soon as I had created the file you began! I am surprised! I'll be right back. Don't go away. I am anxious to hear what you have to say.

I am back. I got myself a cup of chamomile tea to help me relax. I hadn't realized that I was nervous about our talking until I went into the kitchen and wanted to start cleaning! In the past, cleaning has been a distraction, a way to avoid, or maybe an outlet for my nervous energy.

Yes, I understand your coping mechanism.

The purpose for this transmission will be revealed shortly. First, I must explain who I am. I am Letmar. I come from far away land Ketmirh in spacecraft. I travel with many others. We are stationed upwards from your planet many miles. We go undetected for many days. [This could mean a few days or eons.]

My intention with the transmissions is to have [an] exchange with you. I realize that you [are] not but writer and channel. You [do] not understand the ways of the world, but you are able to answer many questions that I have that I can take and expand onward. I will be able to take the information you give to me and go further into my understanding of your culture.

As I have explained in [my] earlier communication I have studied long and tedious hours to learn this way of communication. I speak of your language. I must study your ways.

You know when I think of what you just said. You have studied my ways in order to learn my language; I wonder what else you must know. Because as you study or observe our different interactions and communications with others you surely have learned much about our culture!

You misunderstand, I think. I study you, yes, but not *with* you. I have been given many different pictures in the mind to study your ways. I have not been privileged to interact with your kind until recently. You see I have been given clearance to work with species on intimate level—personal. I speak to you now. I [am] not given the pictures to learn from.

Wait, you told me that you communicated with me from a spacecraft. You are still working through the mind aren't you?

Yes, I work through the mind. But I work with you. We exchange ideas and words. It is two-way communication. Before, I work alone. I see the pictures and observe. I [do] no[t] have the exchange that is required for me to build on. I require offer [your permission] to ask about certain phrases that I hear. To learn to go forward you must have interchange of words.

Connections had to be made with others before I was given permission to work with any of the beings on the Earth plane. You have guidance and protection. Those who protect you must give hand to me [their permission] before I [may] go forward in the transmissions.

Letmar, my guides told me a while ago that I would be receiving visitors from other planets and I would be listening to them and sharing the messages with others. It looks like this is what I am doing…finally.

Yes, they speak of the galactic highways opening. There are many who travel about in this galaxy, not only, but this universe and have stationed their ships in your aerospace waiting for the exchanges to begin on a more profound level.

There have been exchanges for eons, but your people of higher authority work to keep secret, like to wash away this truth like they wash their dirty laundry. To make it known to all of those on the Earth is to change all. Those in power have huge responsibility to the people and they are fearful of what is to occur if they publicly broadcast this information that they know of us, the Federation, and all it ensues. [This is a] big challenge and [a] big endeavor. The changes go slowly. Each cabinet–presidential delegation wishes not to reveal too big. They fear upheaval of the nation and also the turn of every foundation that they know to be true. You see when it is known on the [public] level we see all and I mean ALL will be turned upside down. God's Truths are to be revealed! Travel will change, economy will change. There is no subject that this disclosure will not affect. I work with you another time. ~END OF TRANSMISSION~

⁂

Welcome Letmar. I am sorry I wasn't able to work with you last week. Stuff happened. I ended up going to visit my parents. I had a busy week.

I know of your travels. I am well aware of your travels. Your guides keep me apprised of when it would work best for me to come to join with you and have conversation.

Today, I wish to comment on some information that has passed before you concerning HAARP. Tulró has given you words concerning this. I wish to elaborate on his comments.

I tell you congratulations on your steps upward. I see you are working with new guide.

Thank you, I guess. I don't really know what is happening with my guides. Nathanal has taken leave for a few days and that is all I know.

Well, be it known that I have seen shift in your legions of guides. I see you accessing the knowledge of Light Beings in higher authority—command.

We continue with HAARP. This facility is under cover for government/military agenda to keep within its grasp to manipulate and control the forces of whatever peoples/country it desires. Remember what affects one affects all. The entity of your country has chosen superior location to withhold true reasons for research. The entity [HAARP] speaks in half-truths. There is no trust for this one.

Here I noticed a shift in his dialogue as he was doing better with his grammar and sentence structure.

I am in [an] area outside of your position of radar capabilities to detect. Our position is high above your Earth's surface. We see much as we have spectacular vantage point from here. We see your military and your NASA working in unusual steps. They plan incognito, but all see, all know what they do. There is little left to secrecy. We find it humorous what the countries of your world do in the name of service and security for the people.

My people of Ketmirh are friendly. We are members of the Galactic Federation. We work with many to go forward by finding ways of better technology for ease of travel and communication. These two endeavors are important to universal peace.

I talk of you now. You are in beautiful position having the magic to hear the higher frequencies that your guides use to communicate with and through you. You have accomplished this way well. They speak to us of how they work with you and what their intentions are in allowing you to open to this frequency. We of Ketmirh are the first in long line to speak to you in this way. We realize that you are not of yet in a position to carry forth our transmissions.

Do my guides help you to communicate with me?

Tulró took over and said, "I am helping to translate Letmar's communications to you. He has different way of communicating. There is much to consider with this endeavor."

I have promised you the pictures of my kind and my spacecraft. There is vital information that I wish to share with you. I have artist available tomorrow. Please consider to work with me for a time. ~ Out~

* * *

Letmar here. You have questions today?

Yes, a friend of mine wants to know more about the specifics of your space vehicles. He is really interested in the sizes and the capabilities. I hope it was all right for me to mention our communication to him.

Letmar did not comment on my disclosure to my friend.

Well, of course, this is not my expertise, but I will explain to you what I can—that you may understand. Your mind—this information is foreign and stretches the imagination. Perhaps when you receive too much data at a time your present knowledge or perceived beliefs will override. I say that the information I hold is so vast, you on a conscious level of awareness are unable, at present, to process.

Our spacecraft is [a] structure of material that is foreign to you. Craft is compound of material that you have on the Earth plane but the formula you do not know. Scientists scramble to find secret formula. Make rich to find. Name held in high esteem. Yes? We do not use fossil fuel like you do. Our energy comes from synthetic origin, yes.

You wonder about us using the mind to direct the craft? No, we do not have this capability as of yet. But there are others who do. We have those who study this way. All are in the process of evolving. We wish to learn more advanced technology. This is true.

I talk of the craft. [I] would like to draw picture now. I draw picture. I know it [is] not quality. *[Someone channeled a drawing of a spacecraft very simplistic in quality for me.]* But the talk I give explains some.

You follow direction well. I give you picture of me also.

The picture of Letmar resembled a humanoid in some ways. However, his mouth was completely altered appearing like a round hole. I didn't get enough detail to get his ears but it seemed as if they were much smaller and shaped differently.

You see, I do not have the physical features as you do. I explain that there is a mother ship and secondary ship that will do explorative travels. Also [we] have smaller craft that will do repairs and what not. It view[s the] outside of larger craft as well as transport us to perhaps another ship or destination. This third ship I speak of is small and easy to maneuver about. Also, has capability of high speed. Go undetected most of time. I find it humorous. We watch you people who watch the skies. *[He is speaking of air traffic control people who watch the monitors.]* They see the bleeps on their mighty screens and suspect there are others about, but no believe because they must have the physical sighting to change their belief.

I go now. I [will] work with you another visit. ~OUT~

*   *   *

The following transmission from Letmar.

Big day for me! I go off [mother] ship earlier! So good to get out and look around for a bit.

I indicated that what Letmar meant was that he got off of the mother ship. This was an assumption on my part as he could have meant that he actually got off the ship and walked on the Earth.

Where did you go?
We traveled, on smaller shuttle, a group of us, outwards the expanse of the United States. A rather quick travel, but enjoyable for us. We see the vastness of your areas both the populated and unpopulated areas. There are some beautiful lands under your government. Also, we admire the architecture of some of your buildings. You are technologically advanced somewhat, but we feel you could use guidance in certain areas. The peoples

are some lacking in their awareness of self, we notice this, while others have advanced greatly in their knowing and connection of the heart language. You have many levels of consciousness that you are working with on your planes of physical existence.

I noticed he said planes instead of plane. This may or may not have been intentional on his part.

You are united yet much divided. We wait and watch for the fireworks. They sure to go off at some point! I make joke here, but we believe in order for you to make big change there will be much upheaval.

I ask you if *you* are safe? We see the Earth breathing and expanding somewhat. With that she moves birthing new land or perhaps new oceans.

I don't know what will happen with me or to me, but I have been assured—promised that I will be taken care of always. But I do not know if my physical body will be safe. I have been told that I may be taken aboard a spaceship until the Earth has stabilized. I want to stay here as long as possible. Although, I guess, it doesn't matter where I am because it is what I feel and I create that matters. It is the love that I feel that sustains me.

I Letmar [did] not mean to cause the tears to fall.

It is all right. I am just emotional today.

The spaceship I live in is rather large. There are many who gathered to come on this mission. Your friend, Sam, is correct about the size. I laugh because he is wanting to know much about this way of travel. Even I do not know all as this is not my area of expertise. I [am a] communications expert. This is my field. I leave all other to my comrades. I concentrate on what I do best and what I enjoy.

I observe you, Nakala, you feel too much under…oh, on your plate. I make error. [deep breath]

If you were to come here on our surface would you be able to breathe our air?

Probably not. Your air is not clean. I fear I perish! I breathe the air, but not wish to breathe your air. Some places may be good, but we monitor, expansive, the levels of radiation and other toxic materials that have been emitted into one of your precious energy sources—air. We are much surprised-shocked even that you have allowed yourselves this injury. The people suffer from the poisons—they die from the poisons. Do you not realize the path you are on?

Yes, we are aware that we are breathing and consuming toxic substances, but for the most part, we do not know how to correct what has–is happening.

In addition, our government has created so many laws concerning what we legally can do and can't do that we are, in a sense, imprisoned. We desire to be free yet there are those who mean to do us great harm because all they care about is the almighty dollar—and control.

Change always begins with you on rudimentary level. You do not poison the air on your level and others follow.

How am I poisoning the air?

By creating the waste and disposing of it like you do.

I don't know what to do to change it, other than grow all of my foods and process it all myself. Even then, I would be using so much water (that isn't pure) that I am really at a loss of how to proceed.

This is one of the many reasons I have come to exchange communications. I wish to bring you aboard my spacecraft and teach you.

Letmar's announcement totally took me off-guard. I felt myself literally shrink in terror. Rather than responding to his statement I got up and went into another room. I found myself staring out the window seeing nothing. I really couldn't believe what I had heard. After a few minutes I had calmed down somewhat and was ready to listen to Letmar again.

Well, what you suggested certainly took me by surprise. I felt shocked, fearful, and excited all at once. But really I am not sure that I trust you. Me? Get on a spaceship…with you? I think about all of my responsibilities and wonder, okay, how long would I be gone? What is it you want to teach me? What about my cat, DJ, my friend, Sam, and my personal needs? What about my home? When would this take place? Do you have to get permission from someone to take me aboard? Will my guides be with me?

Yes, I expected you to have much reaction to my desire to bring you aboard. I wish to have you aboard for extended stay. I wish to teach you many things. I wait for a while longer. I see you have trip planned. The cat you must find home for him—other home. You will be traveling much in very near future. Sam [is] not to come. I realize that he is like security to you, but he cannot hear the words. He would not be able to communicate. You would have to relay all to him—this take too much of your time. The house is to be paid for. You will pay in advance your utilities so there will be no concerns for your home. What I propose would take place in the next four months. I arrange time. I do not require permission from others as this is the purpose of our station. Your guides will remain by your side.

What I desire to teach—this is the desire of our nation to show you our way of living. I know you not mechanic or scientist or even theologian, but I will be most admiring of your presence as we both communicators and messengers. We must work to educate the others of what is about in addition to the new advancements that will be taking place if you choose to adopt.

Nakala there are others who are receiving the transmissions also. We must gather many of you to make mark in your consciousness.

Yes, you will endure physical testing to ensure you do not bring aboard any type of ailment or virus. You must be free of any contaminant. Your clothing will be removed and disposed of. After a thorough evaluation is made of any keepsakes, they may or may not be returned to your during stay. Most assuredly all to be returned at time of departure. [Your return home to Earth.]

Your guides are working with you to dissipate all unbeneficial particles in and on your body physical. ~Transmission Complete~

* * *

I, Letmar have come to assist you in your ways. You know not what I wish to help you with as of yet. We are here, many of us, to show you ways to advance in many areas. You not realize what these transmissions are really about.

I guess I have no idea. At first, I thought it was about learning to balance my life in the physical, but with the Earth shifting into a higher vibration I really don't know.

You just now look into your memory and see the cell dividing like this into two separate entities. This is truth. You will be living on a new and wondrous planet. Yes? The truth be told—yes, I see the Sam fellow. We would like to work with him also.

I wondered if Letmar were speaking in riddles or with symbolism concerning the division of the Earth, but said nothing.

How can you work with Sam? Would I be in this endeavor somehow?

We like his communication skills. He is able to bring out in people the inner. This is strong focused skill. I know not how to speak on this subject with you.

I go back to our conversation concerning the division of the planet into two separate entities. They will be identical yet distinct. I explain to you. The vibrations will be the same. You are dividing the cells just like in the human body. You are creating new—birthing. Yes we speak of the sacred geometry.

What is the purpose of this division?

Evolution: to bring about change. As a universe we continue to grow—to create—to make better—to go higher.

The two planets will yield the energies that you put forth. You like so many will choose to go into a state of love and gratitude while others will remain entrapped in a state of fear. You will be separated and the energies will burst forth with a great momentum allowing you to rise above the 3rd dimension quickly. You think this is speculation? No. We have seen this happen time and time again. It will happen again with this planet.

Will our solar system birth a new sun and a new moon also? Will the two planets know about each other and see each other?

No. We not speak of this now.

I thought we were just going for a polar shift and a shift into a higher consciousness.

All to occur. Yes. We are getting off subject here. I [am] here to teach you about such matters, but choose to do this in my rhythm. I ask you to come aboard my craft. I hear that you decide it all joke or perhaps we test you. More accurate your own guides test you in some manner. No joke, I use simple way. I speak truth. I wish you to look at possibilities concerning this gift.

At this point the red flags were quite visible. I did not feel comfortable with what he was saying about the Earth's division. None of it made sense. I wanted to back off but instead stayed with it and continued on with the conversation.

Letmar, I do not have enough information to assimilate a logical choice in your offer.

We wish to teach you along with several others in many areas. Technology, the workings of the crystals and the plants: you know not the gifts that they offer you. They all have a story to tell and information to carry you forth. We wish to teach you to communicate once again with all of creation through the mind. Your guides presented this material long ago. We go forward in this path if you allow. We [are] advanced beings. We communicate to all and gift each other with our love and abilities. Do I make clear?

Yes, I believe so. How do we go forward from here?

At this point I felt torn. I was weighing the options as I could assimilate them. Meanwhile, my aim was to keep Letmar connected and communicating so he would continue to give me more information. Something about all of this just didn't feel correct. However, as I reviewed the idea of leaving all my worldly responsibilities behind the idea sounded very attractive, tempting even. If I could just let it all go… However, I just didn't think I could to make it happen. Perhaps Letmar just didn't have the ability to convince me that this was an idea that I should move on. Perhaps this simply wasn't something that wasn't part of my contract, so I made excuses.

Again I looked at it from the angle that it would be so nice to just walk away from all of my responsibilities—just go… Although, I felt there may be a high likelihood that I might grow discontented at some point. Maybe I would be like one of those time travelers not having a real job, but just go here and there. How would I make my own way? I have so many questions.

I [will] work to answer you. It will take time for us to learn if this endeavor [is] correct for you. We look at many [potential volunteers]. There are those who have great desire to go forward. As with any movement, you are to receive information to make possible. I see you intrigued, but you know not the details of what you get into. You have good life now, but you see all crumble before so long. No, you continue on as before. The energies continue to climb higher. You continue to go closer to learning how to work your energies in the physical body. There is much work for you to do to come to a point of real understanding. I wanted to bring this possibility to the forefront so we can feel what will be the correct choice for you to make. I hear—am told you wish to become ascended master. Big responsibility for you to serve all. You must learn to relax yourself. We are in no hurry. Go into love and gratitude as your leaders instruct you. No matter the final outcome, I wish you to come on my craft and see for self what is before you.

What you are suggesting sounds awesome. Although, part of me feels like it is crazy to even consider such a thing. I realize how ingrained my programing is—that this Earth is the only place I will live until I pass from my body.

I have been told life on other planets probably doesn't exist. How could it?

It seems my life was almost prearranged—predesigned, if you will, to only fulfill certain roles that may or may not make me happy.

So receiving transmissions from you, a space traveler, has really caused me to contemplate what is really important in my life— what are my priorities?

I see in my preconceived reality, this place, my life is extremely limited! There is so much more! I am asking you to please show me as much as you can and to consider me as a student.

What I say to you now. Listen closely. You have before you vast possibilities, many masters who cater to you. They teach you the ways to communicate with the others—my kind. I am to take you into my physical reality and teach you for a time. You ask what about your home, your family, everything. I say sell your items or dispose of them—leave all behind.

What would I come back to?

You not come back to this place. Perhaps it is time for you to move on—move forward.

What about the books? I agreed to write them with the Akasie… my father, Quem…

Go into mediation and feel what is right for you. Know in your heart space what you must do.

It is like you are dangling an eye-catching piece of chocolate candy in front of me; I can smell the chocolate. I want it! Yet, I question if it is the correct decision—for my highest good? Am I ready for this type of lesson?

There is much to consider. Yes? You would leave behind all.

What dimension are you in?

You hit an important issue. How would you be able to handle a higher frequency? This is a very good question. *[He obviously had read my thoughts on this issue.]* We are at a higher frequency and you would have to adapt. When you are with others of a higher frequency it is disturbing for you. Your guides are working to bring you into alignment with us. It would not be an issue. We are fifth dimensional consciousness, but not limited to this level. We have the capability to enter into your sphere easily and undetected. Fear not.

I ease into your life. I hear your concerns and your questions. We not rush into this. We have a few cycles to consider this.

What I am putting before you is another life change of vast proportions. You go to another lifestyle all different. You have desire for this, but same time you feel maybe too radical for you. You wonder if you would ever see your Earth again or bathe under your cosmic sun; maybe never have the opportunity to gaze into the night's sky to view the stars and the moon and ponder their origin. You think I speak of you being on vessel for a time to teach you. Yes and no. I speak of learning new not really. What I speak of is assisting you in your teachings for your vibration to climb, as well, as [to] gain a higher understanding of all. Yes, like school. This I offer you to attain mastery level to serve in particular area. Yes, you writer, you reader, you messenger.

I wouldn't be needed like that anymore.

Yes! You no understand! You have attained this level of mastery. It is time to go further if you desire. You continue to be servant. Yes, messenger. Your spiritual guides—the masters, what do you think they do? They bring the messages, they are teachers. They are masters. What is it that you are working to attain at this very moment? ~LETMAR OUT~

After that last transmission, Letmar had not approached me again concerning boarding his spacecraft. The next transmission I received from him follows:

DATED OCTOBER 31, 2012

I see you on holiday. The children run the streets in search for the next treasure. We hope, ah, yes, the doorbell rings!

It has been many years since I gave candy out. 1998 I believe was the last year. (We had moved to a rural area after the passing of my son.)

[This is a] joyous occasion. I have spent months preparing myself to communicate with you. Oh, of course with others as well. Now, I feel ready, competent to exchange words with those in the human bodies who speak like you do.

My station is far to the east; directly over a large body of water. No not a lake but the ocean—the Atlantic Ocean closer to the Caribbean Islands. We move outward on our many travels seeking out the Light.

Tonight [there is] much excitement. The children they [are] most happy—Create Light! A bridge for us.

(Someone directed my gaze to a banana and a knife which I was immediately puzzled by.) A bridge? Okay…cut a banana or open the banana to illuminate the light as a bridge. What?

You are not following my thought. I explain. When you cut open fruit—the energy spills outward. Such is the concept when a child laughs—is opened up. The energy spills outward-illuminating from the source.

I desire to connect with you often. Once a week? We set date? We have waited until you were settled in the home. (Letmar was referring to my move to a new location.) There are many of us who desire to speak. ~LETMAR OUT~

The problem here was…I wasn't settled. I was being guided to go to Scotland and then Brazil.

At the time of this transmission I was living near my parents in the Wichita, Kansas area. My next home in Kansas City lasted one year—long enough for me to completely remodel the house and get the message to leave Kansas City during February of 2014 to visit Mt. Shasta, California.

It has been a long string of moves for me—one directly after an-other—just barely getting comfortable and making new friends when my guides would announce that I was to move again. I have been here in California for six months now and pray that I will be guided to stay put for a while.

* * *

I had not heard from Letmar again, not until yesterday that is. He had simply vanished. Possibly, the reason for his disappearance was the fact that I had decided that boarding a spacecraft wasn't what I wanted to do…at least not for now. I imagined that Letmar was profoundly en-gaged in promoting his idea and making arrangements for others to board his craft.

Yesterday, as if passing through Letmar had quickly made himself known, and expressed in a very brief and concise manner that he still desired our connection—our communications. Nothing else was said or shared.

I am receptive to the idea that Letmar desires to continue to want to exchange information, for whatever reason, but a part of me feels over-taxed. Several beings have indicated a strong desire to write through me. It seems that I will be in high-demand for some time.

CHAPTER
THIRTEEN

This morning, I fully expected Letmar to arrive and begin again his valiant efforts to coax me to board his spaceship. This was not to be. My guides had other ideas. Instead, this morning I was directed to get busy with the household chores and have everything in place before I began my day of writing. Boldly, Sakeem had stated that there would be no moments to complete mundane tasks this weekend.

Umm…this was only Thursday. I wondered to myself what my guides had planned. However, I didn't ask that question. I have learned from years of training that asking about future events is futile—pointless—a total waste of my energy. Why make my life more complicated when the future is subject to change? I find it to be that simple.

On countless occasions, I have heard Babaró say, "Please allow us to direct you in your daily movements. Wait until *we* tell you what steps to take." Of course, I ruminated; there is always the issue of listening to my heart in all situations.

I must confess my life has gotten so much easier when I allow my guides to direct me on matters such as when to do my errands or when to call on someone. There is a multitude of areas I follow my guides in. Nonetheless, there are times when *I* will have a great desire to do something and my guides have not mentioned it. This is when *I* move as this to me is a clear indication that I have received an inner prompting: I feel the desire deep in my heart. I have been instructed to always follow my heart: do what makes my heart sing.

Just then I heard Babaró say, "Babaró here, Nakala. How are you feeling?" "Well, to be honest, I find this all perplexing. Last night, being full of energy, I wanted to jump out of bed to write. However, I was directed to stay put and to sleep, which I did. This morning, however, I feel tired—just plain worn out."

"Nakala, what is it that we can do to restore your vigor—assist you in balancing? Get up? Stretch? Get some fresh air? Perhaps something to get your energy moving will help."

Instead of doing as Babaró suggested, though, I went into the laundry room, reached inside the dryer and got an arm-load of clean clothes to put away. As I walked into the bedroom, I saw Trent, through the window. Trent is the cedar tree who stands approximately seventy feet high and lives directly outside my door.

It was as if I heard a tiny voice, a memory of not so long ago. My mother, Sarah's was saying, "Nakala, use your new found appreciation to love the Nature Spirits. Talk to them. Go out and hug a tree and tell the tree your feelings for nature. The tree will share your messages with all of nature as all are One."

Over time, I would learn the importance of loving nature as this is the Golden Mean (bringing together two extremes to find the middle ground).

When I take the time to go outdoors to hug Trent, the connection I feel is total Oneness. My thoughts concerning the mundane (in the physical realm) fade quickly, evaporating into the ethers. The periphery of my vision vanishes. There is nothing else that matters in that single moment. This is to BE in the Now. Immediately, my heart connects to the heart beat of our Mother Earth. My body begins to feel rejuvenated—alive once again.

So why have I not visited Trent in several days, perhaps even as long as a couple of weeks? I can say that it is the cold that keeps me indoors. But is that the only reason—the real reason?

As stepped out of the house and went to Trent and wrapped my arms around him, I heard him ask, "Why must you wait until you are feeling poorly to come to me? Why must you wait?" I shook my head and said, "Probably because I want to get every ounce out of every minute during my day and to come hug you, well, it takes a special effort and it isn't productive."

Trent then said, "Do what feels good. This is your life. Enjoy it." Dismayed, I stepped away from him as I said, "thank you," and came back into the house. I felt so much better, but I was troubled. Really why did I wait to visit Trent? He was merely ten feet from my back door! In order to stay grounded, stepping outdoors and connecting with Trent or another tree was something that would be beneficial and would be a very good idea to do *every single day* no matter what the weather conditions were or what my schedule was. I *knew* how good it made me feel when I did this. So why did I deliberately avoid going out?

Well, there isn't just one answer for my unwillingness. I had created many diversions or excuses to stay indoors.

"The thing is," Babaró began, "You have made many excuses for not going forward in this discipline. The number one reason you do not feel comfortable going outdoors and hugging a tree is you have neighbors about. You are embarrassed to be seen doing something, that to them, may seem peculiar."

Babaró had me all right. I was self-conscious of going out and hugging Trent in case there may be someone around watching.

"Nakala, my dear, hugging trees is nothing new and certainly nothing to be ashamed of. Perhaps someone does see you. What of it? This could make the beginnings of a great conversation; a wonderful opportunity to teach others one way to become and stay grounded, not only, but to love nature!"

PART

SIX

HOLD THE VISION

CHAPTER
FOURTEEN

"Once there was a time when all seemed simple. Now the possibilities are endless," had been Sakeem's opening statement. "Your life was mapped out as a wife, mother, and grandmother who used your time completing household tasks, going to different and amusing events, and making fanciful items for your pleasure. Now your marriage is finished and those items, for the most part, have been laid aside as your attention is strongly fixed on the writings—our messages—your work in the ascension program. You see before you an image—this desire as if you were looking into a mirror. You are to *hold the vision*.

"However, you have weakened a bit; you have looked about and wondered if we, by the mere use of these written words, our messages, are able to take the reader into a place of learning with true integrity. Are we, you ask as a team, able to bring forth even a single topic that resonates true; shifting the reader into the next level of expanded awareness?

"In the beginning you were told that if you repeat our messages, you in essence, own them. This has caused you to view our work (celebration of life through the written word) as a huge weight that you, alone, must carry."

Sakeem had touched on a sensitive topic that I had carefully considered. Presently, I assess all issues brought up in the writing, and I have found that there have been times that I just haven't been knowledgeable in some areas to know for sure that what I have received has 100% integrity.

Sakeem continued, "Through the written works we present, we address particular fears. These fears that I speak of are instilled deep inside of you. One of those fears is through the writings there may come conflict—dishonor somehow.

"There are scores of other writers who address the very same topics as you do, Nakala. I say this: not always will the writer have the very same view nor the very same information. In addition, as a writer, you have a unique way of expressing those views. Laydown your fear as it has the power to debilitate, to weaken, taking hold of you, dragging you down into the muck and the mire. *Hold thy vision* on God's Truth and your faith that where we take you is honorable and just.

"Being a spiritual channel for the Beings who reside in the higher realms hasn't been an easy area of service. Doubt has arisen on many occasions. You ask your questions to us. Is the information you receive absolute truth? You demand there be no discrepancy, no error. We assure you, yet there are times when you still, to this day, question the authenticity of our messages.

"I bring forth this subject matter for reason, not only to appease you, but to teach the reader of a matter of utmost import!

"The matter concerns the disclosure Babaró made concerning his embodiment as Henry Wadsworth Longfellow that was written about in our last book, *In the Light of Day*. The story is compelling in nature and absolute truth.

"Nevertheless, this past week, at a gathering you attended, Nakala, it was causally proclaimed to the group that the Ascended Master Lanello had incarnated as Sir Lancelot and also as your Henry Wadsworth Longfellow. This had been the second time you had heard this tidbit of information. Still the news came in as a blow to your ego and we heard you whimper, "How can that be?" We saw you still yourself—heard your declaration: There must be an error. I will surely find the truth concerning this matter."

Sakeem was determined to assure me and to calm my concerns and continued, "I stood beside you Nakala. You were most determined to get to the bottom of it. Upon arrival to your home that evening, even though it was late of hour, you took your seat at your computer and searched for the answers you sought. This Lanello fellow had pasted a string of intriguing life-streams behind his name that heavily stirred the senses!

Sakeem continued on, "He, this Lanello, had claimed to have embodied as Henry Wadsworth Longfellow. You saw it in black and white. Nakala…what you saw was the writings of another channel that received the information and published it. Having been published, you as all others took it as truth! It was there…written before your very eyes, therefore it had to be the truth. Yes?

"This teaching is multifaceted and for you most beneficial to receive at this exact moment. Upon hearing this data, your doubt rose in visible waves of dense energy. As time carried on so did your suspicion, growing ever stronger to distrust, anger, and fear! You had written on this exact topic and it was due to be edited and published soon! Your honor was/is at stake!

"I give to you this: Babaró gave you this story to teach you many things. The first is he would never fabricate a story to be printed to tarnish your name nor his! Never!

"They spoke of the incarnations of Lanello, well, that was all due to happen for your benefit. It was laid out in advance for you to receive.

"Just recently you have received the understanding that many people in the physical bodies have walk-ins during the life cycle on Earth. You, Nakala, have more than one. These may be explained as God-aspects of your Divine Cosmic Matrix that encompasses your many bodies or another consciousness (another soul) has chosen to embody along-side or instead of the original soul that has taken the flesh form. (This may happen at any time during the life-stream, but after birth.) It matters not as you currently have little understanding to no comprehension of how the Christos operates.

"In other words, there have been many times that two or more souls have inhabited the same body either at the same time or different times. This is not new data. Do I make myself clear on this issue?"

"Well," I hesitated, "the part about 'God-aspects of your Divine Cosmic Matrix that encompasses your many bodies' is not entirely clear to me."

"What I mean by that statement is that you have attributes or facets instilled in your Divine Cosmic Matrix (all that you are) that are of God's Perfection."

"Well, I understand that, but if that particular aspect has reached perfection then why have a walk-in?"

Because, my dear, you are expanding your consciousness. When you reach a particular level of mastery in the scheme of it all your I AM Presence may want to work on another aspect to bring forth perfection in another area that is being expressed through the physical body. This is when another aspect is walked-in or joined or changed in entirety."

"Would you please define aspect so I may understand that term better?"

"Dear One, what I am speaking of may be a myriad of things. It could be a virtue or a skill or a combination thereof. In short, this may occur when you are aligned to expand in some area, but require assistance to attain mastery.

"I speak of another individual consciousness joining the original soul or doing a walk-in by switching consciousness. This is one way for the I AM Presence (the God in you) to evolve through the physical vehicle.

"In your individual case, you have the Ascended Master Samuel Paul who has walked-in and presently shares your consciousness. This is for the purpose to see you through the ascension program. Remember, Dear One, there is always a more expanded understanding. Never assume that you have the entire teaching. There is more to learn always!"

CHAPTER
FIFTEEN

Babaró spoke swiftly as I typed, "As it were, it was announced last eve that you would have a visitor here today. 'Get yourself prepared,' we tell you! To your dismay, we did not reveal the guest's identity. That has remained confidential—a gift until today—now."

I waited for Babaró to continue—to give me a name—some explanation so I could continue to type. However, no words were forthcoming. Instead, there had been several attempts to get a message across to me by guiding me to look at the picture I have on my desk of Adama the High Priest of Telos. Specifically, I was guided to look at his eyes, then the color red. I was a little confused at what Babaró was trying to tell me. My interpretation was the eyes meant to see or watch and red meant energy.

Perplexed, I asked, "You want me to see energy? You want me to watch energy?"

Then suddenly without explanation I knew that Babaró wanted me to look for the energy of my guest. Immediately, I turned around in my swivel chair to face the emerald-green recliner that was located on the other side of my office. There I saw him…the image of Adama.

In a courteous manner, I welcomed Adama and waited for further instruction.

Adama greeted me in a casual manner then said, "I wish to give you a message to be included in this writing.

"In addition, I wish to express my appreciation at your thoughtfulness at your prominent display of my picture there on your desk, in your home. You are to acquire pictures of the Ascended Masters and display them about your home. This will assist in raising the vibration of your home. In turn this will assist the masters when they wish to visit you for any reason."

Fully understanding Adama's directive, I knew it would be best if I had pictures on display of the masters in my home. However, I had just gotten comfortable with the arrangement of my things. I really liked how I had assembled the few items that I had brought from Kansas. Then I remembered this teaching: If you get too comfortable in life you will stop reaching beyond what is directly before you and subsequently you will inhibit growth or stop it entirely.

I stopped and looked around my office and saw a host of framed photographs of my family and remembered another teaching that I had just recently received. Photographs and art as with all things hold a vibration. Then my mind drifted to the odd but persistent directive that I had received for over two weeks to buy some new clothing.

Almost every day Nathanal insisted that I get on a particular Website and order two new pair of jeans and every day I had openly rejected the idea. I kept putting it off because I didn't want to spend the money. I reasoned, I can get by on what I have for the rest of the season without purchasing more clothes!

Then three days ago Nathanal had pleaded with me but his voice held an unusual edge that I don't hear often from him. His voice had taken on a stern quality, a severity even, "Nakala, listen to me! Please buy those pants, now!" He had gone on to say, "We want you to look good and feel good!"

He paused for a few minutes as I thought about my day's tasks before he continued, "You have *no idea* the level of assistance beautiful clothing has on you concerning your vibration!" I had thought to myself. We are talking about a couple of pairs of jeans for crying out loud! That is when I realized the importance of his request that sounded more like a command. Consequentially, I immediately did as he had directed and ordered the pants.

"Yes," Adama said, "all matter vibrates to a particular octave. Because you are consciously seeking to raise your vibration it is time you take responsibility for your actions by being cognizant of what you surround yourself with. All is energy and has an effect on every step in your individual evolution as well as the evolution of the collective.

"As an Emissary of Light you are to be one of the first to acknowledge that in order to expand, you must shift your conscious awareness. In doing so you automatically shift what and who you surround yourself with: what energies you immerse yourself in or vice versa.

"No more will you surround yourself with items that hold a lower frequency. Beauty and order are Heaven's first law. This means clutter is to be vanquished in all areas. To live modestly: this is key. You are to focus on letting go of certain items. I am sure Nathanal will assist."

Again, I perused what was housed on the bookshelves in my office and wondered what on earth I could discard. But then I reminded myself this was not the time to ponder any choices that I may have regarding Adama's message.

"Nakala," Adama resumed his teaching, "you have received this message beforehand. Just not on this level. After time, you will grasp a deeper understanding of certain teachings. You are ready to incorporate, in particular areas, a level of mastery. Know this for it is so.

"I hear your deliberations. Last week you had a small fire here in your office. The top of your oak file-cabinet alongside of your carpet suffered minimal damage. You were able to clean it up satisfactorily. Because of the color of the carpet the burns are scarcely evident and the top of the cabinet now dons on a beautiful hand-crocheted covering. The damage wasn't so extensive that you felt you should file an insurance claim.

"The reason I speak of this is now you have items that are blemished lowering their vibration and in turn the entire room and home. In order to replace items costs money. What has occurred is common place in your society. There are times that items are damaged from one reason or another. It is your choice to make to leave as is, repair, or replace. Nakala look at it like this. With the cabinet the burns disrupted the connective tissue causing an interrupted flow of energy. The finish of the wood was severely distorted and discolored. In other words, the integrity and beauty of the piece has been injured. When you look upon the burned area you go into judgment. You see the imperfection and it makes a mark on your subconscious mind—this is damaged: it is no longer perfect. Your focus is drawn to those imperfections! As you view you are lowering *your* vibration with subtle thoughts."

Thinking that Adama had concluded his message, I respectively thanked him. With a firm tone, he responded, "I am not finished, as of yet. There is one other piece to this. Nakala, you are to lead by example. This means you are to create a space that is sacred. I go back to the pictures of the Ascended Masters. It is time to claim who you are and what you are about." Adama then said, "I must take my leave. I give you thus until another time. ~ADAMA

* * *

Adama's message had made its intended impact. During the night I had woken up several times with information being given to me from masters or my God-Self that was to be implemented in my daily life.

For instance, I was to prepare an altar in my home to place my candles, crystals and other items that are considered sacred. My thoughts raced forward with clarity, so much so that I scoured each room in my home and the furniture accessible for the perfect location to create this sacred space. In my mind, I looked at all of my tables and benches—anything that I could shift into an altar. Nothing seemed suitable. Not finding an answer right away, I simply asked my guides to please assist me in this endeavor and had gone back to sleep.

The other times I had awoke during the night, it was as if I had been discussing certain subjects with the masters or my Higher Self and then been swiftly and accurately propelled back into my physical body at such a speed that I woke up retaining the information to be examined on the lower level of consciousness knowing that I had a mission that was to implemented on that level.

* * *

The next morning, even though I had instructed Nathanal to wake me up at 7:15, I fought getting up and went back to sleep. Then at 8:00 I was awakened. This time, even though I was still tired and felt out of sorts, I found myself leaping out of bed and rushing to my closet to select my clothes for the day.

Someone was working through me that had already set the intentions for the day. I felt like I was on a caffeinated high complete with the jitters. This was not me and I didn't like it. Quickly and accurately, as if all were pre-planned, I reached for a black skirt and a beige top with black dots on it. Then I reached for a black cardigan. In my mind, not expecting an explanation, I wondered what the big rush was. However, in a curt manner, Nathanal said, "if you had gotten up when agreed upon this would not be occurring just now." …Ah, another teaching is it.

Inwardly, I groaned. Slowly I was recalling my itinerary—the long list of To Dos. Today we were to write (Ascended Master Samuel Paul had planned to assist me with the manuscript today). Beforehand, however, there were several things that were to be accomplished. It was time that I pulled myself together so I called my Beloved I AM Presence forth and affirmed that my Divine Cosmic Matrix was in total alignment with itself. I affirmed that I was focused, motivated and full of joy! I saw Nathanal nod his head once in approval as he responded to my declaration, "That is better!"

It amazes me that Samuel Paul is able to stay quiet for days on end. I know he is with me as we share the same body. (He is a walk-in discussed in the previous chapter and yes, I understand the definition of walk-in does not match what Samuel Paul has done.) Does he reside inside of the physical vehicle or perhaps in my aura somehow? Samuel Paul moved my hand to my heart and tapped on it indicating that he was in or connected to my heart. Somehow, Someday, perhaps I will have an understanding of how he is able to share my body.

"First before we go any further," Samuel Paul insisted, "You are to get up and get a snack until your lunch is ready. Your energy wanes." I did as he suggested and immediately felt better.

"We have much to accomplish today—many areas to cover for the purpose to uplift, through our messages, the peoples of the nations.

"Before hand, I acknowledge the rains that have moved in. Your affirmations on having normal weather (precipitation and climate) are taking affect. Your prayers are heard—your gratitude is felt and stored with like affirmations and prayers. Know that the universe responds with statements that are in the now. 'We are receiving the normal rainfall for this area always.' Know this to be the absolute truth!

"Now, Nakala, it is for me to give forth certain information. Your Nathanal and Babaró have taken leave for the day. They are off on a journey that is sure to please. There are days few that the two of them, together, deviate from your side. May it be known I am with you, always.

Samuel Paul had used the words 'I AM' and I wondered if he were giving me a clue. Perhaps his words had a double meaning.

"You ponder the workings of my nature. How I am able to ride with you in this vehicle (your physical body). You know that my vibration is much higher than yours. You believe it to be hardship for me to endure your immature quality. Nakala, I am here to assist you on your sacred journey as there are many others who have given their lives over in ser-vice as well. Know that I am able, willing, and most certainly without question or doubt, here to assist you on your journey. It is my *pleasure* to share this ride with you.

"You are next in line as Queen of Myra, Pleiades. It behooves me to attend to Your Grace at this time. Let the training commence! You see, Nakala you are not only in training to take over leadership in Myra alongside of your beloved Nathanal, but you are in the ascen-sion program. Just now there is much for you to grasp on the lower level of consciousness.

"Nakala, all Masters of Light, be them ascended or not, are constantly vigilant of their energy. Many go to the Temples to *recharge*, not only, but to give forth in concentrated efforts or forces to the Cosmos. I, as well, attend. You wonder how I am able to serve you and travel to the temple as well. I give it to you. Nakala, you and I are inseparable. Honey, check yourself. I feel the fear rise from your emotional bodies."

"Wait. You said, 'emotional bodies'. There is more than one?"
"Nakala, you know not who you are. You know not what you are comprised of. Your Divine Cosmic Body or Matrix is immense—complex. We give unto you small steps to ease the never-ceasing thirst for understanding and wisdom.

"Now, I must move on. The teachings aren't to wait for you and your Earthly counterparts. I would like it very much if I were granted space in this manuscript for introduction. I am Pleiadian and an Ascended Master. This means that I came to the Earth and lived out a peaceful existence for a number of years…that is until the ego was invited to take command. Slowly we descended into the abyss that so many refer to as The Fall. It was all part of the plan as it was part of evolution. The Earth is not the only planet of which has experienced this shift or spiral downward or this shift or spiral upward.

"There are literally millions of Ascended Masters who are in wait of students. At this moment, you have at least five Ascended Masters at the ready to serve you! This is what we do, *serve you*! We shall continue to serve you until each and every one of you ascends as well. That is our pledge to you."

"Samuel Paul it seems there are many of the people here who don't give a lick about their spiritual nature. How many more eons will it take to rouse these bohemians from their sleep?"

But I knew his answer really didn't matter as there was something deep within propelling them forward to inform and teach those who decidedly remain in the dark concerning their Divine essence. I felt it as well.

Then I was reminded, "Nakala look to the good in all beings."

CHAPTER
SIXTEEN

Today Nathanal suggested that I take my crazy quilt that has been "in progress" for several years out of storage. Already, I have several blocks completed that I have incorporated luxurious fabrics like velvets, satins, silks, and taffetas with bits of antiques lace here and there. The effect is rather stunning.

At first, I balked at Nathanal's idea. I knew what a complete mess I'd be looking at with all the fabrics, sewing machine, ironing board and another table to cut the fabric on. When I get going with the fabrics it can appear rather disorganized in a few hours. I simply didn't want to look at it when I wasn't working on it.

However, after a few days of considering Nathanal's recommendation, I reasoned that I can just shut the door until I am ready to work on the project again.

But instead of getting up and getting set up with the project and sewing the quilt blocks Saturday morning like I had planned, I was directed to drive to Redding an hour south of here. I wasn't into the idea at all. I questioned why I should go. There was nothing I wanted to buy. No sights I wanted to see. My heart simply was not into the adventure and I was very determined to express my feelings on the matter.

It was as if what I said had not been heard and certainly not considered. Nathanal had persisted with his scheme to the point of basically begging me to get myself ready and head out. I wondered if this was one of those times when I was to put my foot down and say 'no,' I just want to stay home and make something beautiful and rest.

Over time Nathanal wore me down: I gave in to his seemingly unlimited display of endurance by getting ready and getting into the car and driving south. My energy level was down and I had difficulty maintaining a good attitude. Basically, I griped and complained the entire way. I just wasn't able to see the sense in driving an hour away to a major city on Saturday.

As if to pacify me, Nathanal promised that the first thing we did upon arriving in Redding would be to find a restaurant for me to have lunch at. He had added in a real sweet persuasive tone…a restaurant that serves healthy meals.

Eating seemed to help my mood quite a bit, although that didn't last long. I was told the objective of the trip was to find me a navy blue sweater, some gifts for my grandkids, and some loose-leaf Jasmine tea. Oh yes, Nathanal had baited me with the bead store as well. So after looking for a non-existent navy blue cardigan I drove to the bead store. At least there, I was in an atmosphere of creativity. Then I drove on to the co-op for the tea. Finally, I said to Nathanal, "Look, I have had enough. I am going home."

But on the way home Nathanal asked me, "What about those giant pine cones you want for the faerie houses?" Ah, now he that he had caught my attention. I had wanted to build the faeries a house or two. I was willing to try using the scales or plates from the pine cones for the shingles on the houses. My aim was to begin communications with the Elemental Kingdom (AKA the Nature Kingdom). I figured what better way to introduce myself than to build them a house?

Nathanal directed me to get off at a particular exit and take a frontage road. He took me to a dirt turn-off taking me into a cloister with a well-travel path large enough for vehicles. I felt like I was trespassing but drove on in anyway. The trees blocked the view from the road so I was hidden. Just a few feet in I saw them: dozens of freakishly enormous pine cones. (Which I know now are called sugar pine cones.) They were lying on the ground amidst heaps of trash! I was appalled—sickened that people were using this clearing as a dump.

Logically, there was nothing I could do about the debris as I did not have a truck or any trash bags. The thicket and its treasure-trove of trash were quite undetectable from the road. Desperately, I tried to shield myself from the disturbing site before me by keeping a tight focus on the delight of gathering a few pine cones to incorporate into gifts for the faeries.

Nathanal obviously wanted me to see that area. I am not sure why. At the time, I had felt compelled to begin to pick up the trash but knowing that I had no place to put it immediately disregarded the impulse.

But the image had made its statement loud and clear and boldly imprinted in my mind's eye that the area was in serious need of some TLC.

For now, though, without further investigation there is nothing I can do.

I felt like I was missing some important piece of the lesson and waited for clarification. No one spoke. "Okay," I said, "What am I missing here?"

"Nakala, remember the lesson on holding the vision of Heaven on Earth? Remember that you are to envision what your idea of a perfect Earth looks like?"

"Well, of course Nathanal," I replied, "What does this have to do with that parcel of land?"

"Envision that land being pristine. Love that area and know that the correct custodians are being summoned to take over and care for it properly. See it in your mind as perfect!"

I cleared my mind ready for the next subject to write on. However, Nathanal motioned that we were not ready to move forward yet. He guided my vision to the pink ceramic fish my daughter had made me while attending grade school saying, "Either you sink or swim." I sat for several minutes contemplating his riddle. At first, I thought he was referring to the collective: either we get it together or get off the planet.

Not knowing how to proceed, I studied the possibilities. What could I do to assist with the clean-up of this land? I could find out who owns that land. But then what? I don't have the resources to clean it up and keep it clean. The people who were using it for their dump aren't considering the Earth as a valuable resource. They either didn't have the resources themselves to take their trash to the appropriate site or they just didn't give a care. In either case, they would continue to use this place or another place to dispose of their garbage until their awareness changed or they were forced to stop. I, for one, can't keep people from dumping their trash there or anywhere else. My attempts would be futile and pointless. Unless these people changed, they would continue to find a place to dump their garbage.

I stopped, inviting Nathanal to elaborate on his idea. In turn he waited for me to examine all sides of the situation. I am to hold the vision of a pristine clearing—a clearing that would please all life? But still this is not what is required to get people to see the higher road. People must change first! They must learn that the Earth has a consciousness just like them. We all want to be respected, loved, and cherished.

I saw Nathanal give a single nod and whispered, "Yes." Then he added, "You are not powerless in this situation. Quite the contrary, you are to add these people and this Earth to your prayers and your affirmations." Then Nathanal said something that took me completely by surprise, "Get the code."

✳ ✳ ✳

While I had been introduced to the concept of shifting energy with codes, I had not been given the teachings concerning them to a degree that I felt comfortable using them. I just didn't understand exactly how to work with the codes—I had not yet acquired the correct steps—the protocol. So for Nathanal to direct me to "Get the Codes," motivated me a bit in finding out more about them.

However, when I asked Ascended Master Saint Germain about the codes he instructed me to talk to two people, one I had recently met in Mt. Shasta. Saint Germain had said, "Talk to both of these individuals. Take accurate notes. You are to record all questions and answers verbatim. You are to include your findings in a text.

The first person Germain had directed me to speak to was Crystal, my Pleiadian sister. Crystal had brought up the concept in the first place and the second was a man, Raymond who led a decree group every week in Mt. Shasta.

But why, oh, why wouldn't Saint Germain just answer my questions directly?

After a few minutes of mulling over Saint Germain's directive, I decided to contact Ascended Master El Morya to see what he had to say. Of course El Morya, told me to do the very same thing as Saint Germain. So I got my pendulum out and asked if it would be my highest good to call these people. Part of me felt quite inadequate because the masters wouldn't just give me the information that I sought.

Suddenly, I heard Babaró say, "I speak. Nakala, you are being directed to collaborate with these people concerning the codes. This in turn will teach those who choose to be involved, and at the same time stimulate your minds to seek higher levels of illumination and wisdom. You will have the opportunity to throw out ideas with each other—formulate questions. All of you are at the level that you take these codes as serious business and desire to use them in accordance to God's Will. We teach in a multitude of ways. We desire for you to learn in a way that is fun! You will be much more receptive to implementing the protocols once you receive in fullness and in addition much more committed and disciplined as instruments of Light with this method as each of you are to be involved in all levels of the game. I say, in conclusion, that this teaching is multifaceted and will evolve as you go through the steps. Remember one step leads to another."

Unfortunately, both parties were unavailable.

CHAPTER
SEVENTEEN

This morning as I rose from my warm comfortable bed one of the first things I did was look outdoors to see Mt. Shasta. This morning, however the trees were shrouded in a misty fog that made my enchanted forest seem even more mystical—surreal. As it were, Mt. Shasta was hidden—concealed—unseen to those of us who looked.

During my day I experienced little flashes of energy when I felt like I was participating in a fantastic dream that often heightened into an erotic dance with God. Not in a sexy way but as an exchange of energy with God and that definitely turns me on in a spiritual sense.

As I examine where I am at in this moment I am easily able to recognize the feelings of gratitude for what God has granted me. I truly feel blessed to be participating in this journey on Earth.

Five months have passed since I *landed* in California. In one instant, it seemed, I had been plucked from one world to suddenly find myself in an entirely different world. Quite literally it seems that I have been taken by the hand of God and dropped in this place. It is as if I imagined the entire trip—all the effort it took to get here.

Most members of my family seem to have adapted—accepted my decision to forge ahead to new uncharted land and even forgiven me.

* * *

Abruptly, in my mind, I heard sounds of fabric rustling as if someone were restless, rearranging their position, or possibly wanted to catch my attention.

Without explanation the sound shifted into the image of the lower half of a woman dressed in a cotton navy-blue and white checkered square dance skirt; her petticoat white with navy lace edging. The image expanded for me to see her simple white cotton eyelet blouse with short puffy sleeves. The entire time she kicked her feet to the rhythm of western music that I did not hear. I saw her naked youthful legs. Then I saw her—the totality of her physical being: Her creamy white skin, her glossy red lips and her shoulder-length curly blond hair fashioned to frame her flawless oval face. She wore black tap shoes. Odd…I would have thought that she would have worn boots. The image persisted, her movements uninterrupted. She sure was having a good time…who ever she was. My imagination had taken flight and my joy grew as I watched her go!

Then the image shifted and I caught the image of genderless person stamping his foot; his or her arms crossed over the chest. Like a mime dressed in black with a white painted face, his movements were exaggerated. I burst out laughing as I realized, yet again, Tulró had made his grand entrance.

Tulró! He flits in and out as the mood strikes or perhaps as he perseveres with his teachings. One never knew for certain if a new guide had arrived or if it was Tulró incognito. Because of his teaching style it was always questionable: what was his ulterior motive?

I describe Tulró as the clown of the Akasie family. It seems his mastery at clown-hood supersedes his credentials as an ascended master.

Tulró had decided to let me describe my inner-most thoughts about him before he began to channel—not in the ordinary sense though. Tulró was directing thought forms in my mind as if they were my own. Curious how that is done.

"Really," Tulró intercepted, "in what way would you rather be known? As a clown who has the ability to outwit his unsuspecting students of Light (or even colleagues) or as a dull ascended master, who by the way, can be detected with one eye shut, his movements, way in advance."

I shook my head disbelieving what I had heard. My laughter was so loud that I was conscious that possibly my neighbors had heard me! Even so, I roared at Tulró's wit and his audacity! Would he dare to promote publication of his statement?

I had to admit Tulró had the ability to keep me guessing and in addition he was skilled, so much so, that there was never a dull moment when he was present. His clever disguises suit him well like an extroverted character who indelibly thrives when on center stage. He is sure to generate a lasting impact in a sly but humorous way. To sum it up, Tulró, without holding back, gives himself over to enrich the lives of others on a whole other level.

Then I heard Tulró say in a distinct southern drawl, "I like it! This is who I am. I want it to stay." (In reference to the above description of his character.) And so it shall remain.

At once Tulró distracted me from my writing and said, "I haven't seen you for a time."

I was ready to shut down my computer for a while and have a little chat with him, catch up a bit. However, Tulró pointed to the computer screen and commanded me, "Write, Missy."

"Evidently, Tulró, you have something worthwhile to share?"

"Indeed I do! For years you have questioned my mastery. I kept you on a perpetual edge as to my true identity. Even now, possibly you are kept in the dark?" (I saw Tulró throw his head back as he laughed at his own joke.)

"It matters not as what I have created is a relationship with you and others. You must know your true self in order to pass *my* class. In order to proceed to the next level, you must always acknowledge and follow your true desires (the desire of the heart). Never are you to feel guilt or shame for this desire! I have been known to taunt you into partaking in all sorts of behaviors that you questioned. You simply followed my directive thinking that I knew best.

"True I did/do know best. It took a time for me to get the most important lesson across. You remember that saying, "quality versus quantity"? Now, dear Nakala, you know best as well. Because of the way I chose to teach you, you have awakened from within a strong knowing—a power of who you are directly linked to your sense of self-worth. From now on you will always and forever listen to your heart and follow it."

* * *

"You expect another to come and give you the words—the dictation? I stay on," Tulró announced before he continued his say. "It is yours to know that I requested this time with you to further explain a few things to you. For you, many teachings have gone full-circle. You are being advanced to the next step."

"It is known by some that at the beginning of each year, not only, there are those in the spiritual laboratory (hierarchy) who conducts assessments if it is required. (Tulró meant, that as a rule, assessments are given at the beginning of the year but may be conducted at other times of the year as well depending on the status of the student.) Take it to be like a year-long class. You are tested to see if you will move to the next level on or remain in the same class. Your lessons are planned accordingly.

"Those who are in the ascension program are always assessed during the ending of a cycle and the beginning of a new one. The lessons are packaged, shall we say, to the liking of your Higher Self.

"Always your free-will comes into play but when all is on track and it is seen there is a definite shift in honoring God's Will instead of your own will (the ego's self-centered demand to satisfy the lower bodies) there are scheduled assessments.

"It is with these words that I reveal you have had assessments many times over. When you first learned of this activity you presented yourself like a tiny mouse—small, timid, and afraid or quite the opposite: the ego puffed up with the realization that you were being given an overview. This perhaps made you feel more important? You presented yourself as other than your genuine Self. You worked to please those who wrote the reports! No more do we see this presumptuous state of affairs during assessments! Know that the council is pleased with your progress.

"Ah, I hear you ask if this information is anyone's business other than ours? Make it known there is reason good for this disclosure. There is no need or desire from anyone on your team that you pretend to be of another quality or level. You are perfect in God's eyes as you are created in His Image. You are God's creative expression manifest in the physical form. Look at yourself in the mirror and know that you are God manifest! You are to hold that vision strong and true. When you place yourself in a periphery: watching your outer self from the inner it is as if you are two people. You, consequentially, raise your expectations of yourself and also raise the results of your mastery. Soon you will have integrated the two as one!"

"Thank you, Tulró, for this teaching."

Tulró said in a voice that yielded a humble side to him, "You are so welcome."

To my right, I could see Tulró rise from his seat and smooth out the creases in his robe and turn to leave. But he faltered for a moment and faced me once again. "Nakala, one more thing, when we have a new student (one who has awakened) and consciously desires to celebrate life beside us there are many who raise their voices to the heavens in gratitude and JOY!" Then Tulró turned to take his leave and disappeared.

CHAPTER
EIGHTEEN

As I was doing my daily chores, I moved about the house with efficiency and ease. I had been focused on getting the coffee table cleaned off—just tidied up a bit before I settled in for my day of writing. I had reached down to move over a brass plate full of amethyst crystals and at that precise moment *it* happened.

Fortunately, the couch was right behind me to sink down into—to embrace me—as if the couch had been waiting for this exact moment to support me during a time of uncertainty.

It had happened swiftly without any previous warning. It was as if I had been watching a really interesting TV show and had been totally absorbed in the unfolding drama. Then suddenly, without notice, something snapped: the audio totally shut down. As if by Divine intervention, there were no other sounds coming from the room, the house, or even from the outdoors. In my inner-ear I had heard a sharp hum and then a shrill pop like when a radio station is being tuned in to; then the dial was unexpectedly shut off. At that precise moment in time, it was as if a canopy or shield of sorts had dropped down and around me to deflect all the constant bombardment of sound.

As it happened, I did not panic. I didn't feel any fear that I had lost my hearing—or that I had become disabled. I merely waited for this abrupt and unexplained condition to end. But still, the event had been dramatic and disconcerting.

Whenever something unusual or just plain weird happens, if I can, I stop whatever I am doing. There may be some sort of message that is about to come through or perhaps it may be a clue that I should pay attention to as it may be part of a teaching. My aim is to be with *it* whatever *it* may be. This time had been no exception.

With the back of my legs I had felt for the couch and slowly lowered my body down allowing the couch to accept my weight and comfort me through this experience.

As I sat there, I felt a sense of being cut-off from the world but in the same token I felt connected and alive. I waited for what seemed to be several minutes, but in reality I am sure it had been only a few moments.

In those few moments, I sat on the edge of the cushion. Perhaps this was symbolic of the way I felt internally: on edge.

During the time of absolute silence, I felt the presence of God in a profound and lasting fashion.

My hearing had simply, shall we say, come back into focus or on-line with a similar tuning-in that I had observed when the audio had shut down.

After the episode I wondered if I had experienced some sort of download or activation. Most definitely, my guides had heard my questions but their choice at the time was to not address them. Sooner or later, I would find out what the reason for the incident had been.

Because of this undertow of energy, a memory of a prior incident had been knocked loose which also was a bit on the strange side. A few weeks prior, I had been in bed, my body totally relaxed. I was graciously sliding into a deep sleep. However, my mind was still busy. Before bed I had played one too many rounds of a computer game. As I lay in bed, my mind continued to select the different colors and shapes together to earn points. During the game, I had suddenly experienced what I'd call a black-out. My screen, like a TV screen, that I watched in my mind had shut completely off with a swift click! With the maneuver, I felt almost as if I had been slapped, jerking me into a state of high alert—no longer on the cusp of sleep.

Incredulously, I had asked, "What happened?" It was Samuel Paul who had answered, "I was showing you a little something…what I could do."

That event had shaken me but also had broadened my scope of awareness. It was if my computer screen or the imagery that my mind uses (imagination) had been temporarily knocked off-line (or in this case taken down). The affair had made a lasting impression on me just like the episode where all sound was shut off. It seems incredible that something of that sort of thing may happen. My take on it? It is certainly interesting to be me. But I still wonder what the reason was for the experience.

My question had been heard by someone of higher authority as I began to feel the stirrings. My vibration quickened as I responded to the emotions of comfort and love that took me, enveloped me, in its sweet embrace. I felt a constricting pressure take hold of my chest, (like the proverbial elephant, on the TV ad, that sits down on the man's chest). Because of the intense force I deliberately took in several deep breaths of air.

It was as if I was being transported into another dimension. Who was working with me? Tulró had taken his leave. I asked if it were Samuel Paul who was getting ready to speak but instead I heard the name, "Quem," being said.

My father, Quem… Tears sprang to my eyes. Oh, how, I miss the daily conversations and teachings with him and my mother, Sarah. At once I heard a high pitched sound in my right ear get louder and then shift into a quieter tone that remained constant.

"Yes, my daughter, I have come to your side. Remember the words you received this morn? 'You are to receive something special today.' You dismissed the message saying, every day, for you, is special. True, it is. We are training you to look for the good in all and to expect each and every day to be extraordinary!

"There are days, many, when your mother or I chose not communicate on this level—your lower conscious level. Even so, with you, we are in absolute communication always. When we think of you, you receive this frequency and it is felt in your body as a vibration. Oft times you receive our love, not realizing whence it comes. The same holds true as when you think of us. We always know your thoughts as they come to us swiftly, accurately, and in entirety. How sweet they are, my Nakala."

"Now, I give to you my expertise to answer your questions. During ascension of said person there may be times, many, of unexplained transitory phenomena. It is to be expected that said person undergo initiation which will include, not only auditory, optical, and tactile heightened awareness. Said person is stepping forward into a transcendent illumination. In other words, you are in transition from one consciousness to a higher or expanded consciousness.

"Nakala, during your shifts you have experienced many skillful presentations from the angels, ascended masters, guides, and your Holy Christ Self or your Higher Self all for the sake of communication and assistance as you traverse to the higher realities—ultimately the complete union with your Divine I AM Presence—your God-Self."

"When your abilities to receive audio transmissions with the outer world and even your inner world were temporarily severed it was a period of transition…an indicator of sorts that you had reached a step in your progress and the summation is you had to adjust on a physical level—the brain was required to reset to higher frequencies, of which you experienced directly. This is not to say that all people will experience the same. Fear not as each individual is unique and as such will experience unique.

"Samuel Paul is one of your walk-ins. He remains connected with you at all times. He stands at the ready always! There will be times that he chooses to disclose or gift you with a teaching that is not given in words but as a first-hand experience. Oft times the event will have a heightened and lasting impact on your belief system: meaning to be a participant will instantly shift your belief whereas words must be repeated again and again to make mark strong; even then doubt is often detected. For eons, as a collective, you have operated from the lower consciousness incorporating the opinion that seeing is believing. You, Nakala, for one, are no longer included in that mindset.

"In the sequential incident of your screen being wiped clear in a single definitive instant and it not being done by your own consciousness was merely something that Samuel Paul felt you should encounter because oft times there are things that defy your common reality. To sum it up…Samuel Paul wanted to shake things…*you* up a bit by stimulating the mind; expand your ownership of enfolding and infinite possibilities."

* * *

"Whither I goest, I will go. In search of promise you have entered into an agreement. The agreement I speak of is your scared contract that of which you testified to before you entered into the physical kingdom once again. The agreement was made to your Beloved I AM Presence and to a host of other beings of grand mastery. You are now aware of these beings of which you have placed your trust in and have pledged to honor in all your days forthcoming."

No one had identified themselves or claimed ownership to the dictation that was coming forth. I asked who was giving me the words to type. I heard nothing.

"It is this Presence (your God-Self) that guides you and has patiently waited for eons until you at last bow down prostrate before it in surrender to Divine Service. This Presence—your Presence—desires only to glorify the Creator-the Holy One, through one of its many expressions (you): this is the function of the Presence."

"You were created as an extension—another aspect of the Presence to learn as it expands and evolves. You have been birthed, if you will, into a human vehicle for the Divine Presence to express, learn, and magnify its good, its purpose through.

"The road has been long—arduous. For eons you have been caught-up—distracted by the world of form. You and your brothers and sisters erected an elaborate wall—the veil that left you in the darkness as you had forgotten your true essence—God-Self which is Light.

"Now is the time to place your Divine Attention on your I AM Presence and listen to your heart and follow its prompting. Your Presence has a Divine Plan, Nakala. The Presence is your God-Self. Through the Presence anything is possible as you are a limitless, eternal Being of Light.

"I am Martin. I have come for you in this time as you have stepped forward out of the shadows that were created such a long time ago."

I was surprised that Martin had waited until now in the dictation to reveal his identity.

Martin Sinclair Akasie had been visiting me on and off for as long as I have been able to hear the guides speak to me and through me. Martin is an Ascended Master and it seems that he has been checking up on me for years…for what reason I don't know. He has always been pleasant, even friendly, like a jovial elder who doesn't get in your business but instead comes for a friendly visit. I am sure he is watching out for me in some capacity as I am one of the younger less experienced ones.

Martin as you can see by his name is a member of the Akasie Family. As I said before he is an elder, meaning he is wiser—more experienced and is older like my father, Quem, or even possibly as old as Quem's father who I have been instructed to address as Grandfather Adede.

Taking the title of an Ascended Master indicates he has embodied on the Earth endeavoring to achieve Oneness with all of creation: his God-Self. He has achieved that state. Not having anything else to say concerning Martin, I called out and said, "I am ready for you to take over." Then I felt this tender, sweet energy take hold and I thought I may cry.

"I am Martin, elder brother to your father, Quem. I telepathically read your thoughts. You wonder why Quem was selected to step up as King of Myra when Grandfather Adede stepped down last year. I'll tell you why. As an ascended master it was decided that I would work with those who were in the ascension program as I have gained much expertise in that area.

"Be it known that your father has always been more suitable and agreeable with the placement as head council in the Kingdom of Myra. Just as Nathanal and you are more suited to the position of King and Queen than your brothers and sisters are. You and Nathanal, both, as twin flames, excel in these types of services. It has been duly noted time and time again and recognized as such."

I couldn't say that I agreed with Martin on that count. However, I have taken leadership roles during this lifetime and thoroughly found them both challenging, exhilarating, and even liberating!

"I go on," Martin said. Reading my questions Martin answered, 'Yes, I am member of the group Telbar organized to specifically oversee your ascension and also one of the directors of the Comterous group affiliated with your writings. You wonder why I pop in every once in a while. This is why: I am directly involved in what you are about!"

I shook my head in amazement and asked in a somewhat incredulous even sarcastic tone, "Who isn't involved? I mean, does it take this many masters to get a few books off the ground and in the hands of our readers?"

Martin's tone softened as he answered my questions, "Nakala, you must realize that we are a large family and yes, it does take many masters to make impact large on the masses. There are many positions to fill— many areas to cover. We have our own lives as well. We do not teach students or write and edit manuscripts twenty-four hours a day. Make it known we enjoy other areas of life as well. There are connections to make; meetings to attend. There are family members to visit or travel with. The list goes on! Our service is much like yours only we hold more Light—we are able to serve in an expanded state of Oneness."

CHAPTER
NINETEEN

The week had been full of activity. To have the weekend just on the cusp sounded wonderful. I wanted to relax. Earlier, last month I had been told to pull-in my energy and finish all projects. (I like to do needle-crafts.) So I pulled out a couple of projects that I wanted to finish. Saturday came. I picked a sewing project thinking that I would have several hours to sit and work in a nice leisurely mode.

When I had been in Iowa I had purchase a small quilted bag kit that included the cotton gingham fabric but nothing else. I soon discovered that I didn't have all of the supplies required to finish it. I continued to cut the pieces according to the directions until I could no longer continue without the additional fabric and batting. It really didn't matter to me, though. I could pick up another project that would be just as relaxing.

As the hours ticked by, I began hearing Nathanal and Babaró say that they'd like to go to Medford, Oregon the next day. Medford is around eighty miles north and the highway meanders through mountain passes which can be extremely unpredictable when it comes to forecasting the weather.

At the mere mention of getting in the car and doing yet another road trip I felt my energy plummet to the point of becoming depressed. I felt rebellious and even angry that they would want to take me from a weekend of relaxation. Also, during this time of year, it could be 50 degrees here while north of here through the passes it could be below freezing and dumping snow and ice.

Before I realized it the day was gone. I hoped and prayed that the next day the guides would have decided that to stay home would be best.

Sunday morning I woke up feeling refreshed and went about my day as if nothing out of the ordinary was happening and got ready to do my disciplines (prayers and affirmations). During the previous night I had shifted my perspective and was fine with staying home or going north to the big city.

Every Sunday morning at 9:00 was reserved to meet with Father Quem and Mother Sarah. As a family, we have made that our special time to give thanks for life. Long ago my guides told me that Sunday was family day—that I was to use that day to connect with family and friends and have a good time—do things that I considered to be fun. So when I had set aside that day to write letters, make phone calls or even have gatherings at my home turned into a day to go shopping I usually don't understand their reasoning—am taken aback—not appreciative to why my guides would put this idea in my mind to travel instead of what I had planned. They had plainly told me to pull in my energy—finish all projects…yet?

Secretly, I hoped that my guides wouldn't mention the trip again but if they did, hey, I was okay with it.

Directly, after my meeting with my Pleiadian parents the first thing that Nathanal said to me was, "Get ready to leave. We are going to Medford. Get on your computer and look up some addresses. We are going to Michaels, JoAnn's, and The Craft Warehouse. Also, print out the coupons you find."

I did as told but all the while wondered why they were sending me to craft stores to get more supplies when I was to finish all projects. I also wondered why they just didn't show me which roads to take as well. I knew that they were well aware of the locations of these stores.

Being determined to be well-prepared in advance for the drive and not cave into physical impulses by stopping at Taco Bell when I got hungry I dug out some fresh veggies and prepared them to take with me. Then I decided to bag up some raw nuts as well. As I walked toward the garage door, I grabbed my purse and jacket and headed for Sarah Jane Blue, my car.

There had been talk of getting some canvasses and oil paints for this summer. I thought I was getting a better idea of what the guides wanted me to do. Of course, to take advantage of the sales at the craft stores was smart. I relaxed a bit more at the idea of spending the entire afternoon out shopping instead of staying home and finishing a project. At least now I had a logical reason for the trip, sort of. But still I wanted to know why I had been told to finish all projects but yet was being directed to buy supplies for painting. None of this made sense to me, but then I remembered who I work with. There are many times that it is best that I let go and just trust my guidance.

All of a sudden, I felt a shift in energy. The pressure in my chest had become more intense. Then I heard Babaró say he wanted to take over. Consciously, I steadied my breath as he moved into alignment to write through me. My hands dropped to my sides as my mind emptied. I surrendered—stopped writing—stopped wondering why.

"Yes, exactly," Babaró's remarked as if it had taken me literally centuries to get *it*. I burst out laughing because that is the sort of thing I do: wonder, analyze, and calculate. I wanted to know why the masters—my guides do the things they do. I mean, really, can you blame me?

In my inner vision, I could see Babaró, with his white eyebrows arched, shake his head in an agreeable fashion and repeat his words, "Yes, exactly."

Then Babaró continued, "Be it known, with our directives there is never just one reason for any teaching as they are always strategic and multifaceted. You may grasp a few of our reasons but never in entirety will you have final comprehension as we are accessing many levels of consciousness as we traverse about. You simply are not at the conscious level to grasp the entirety of what and why we do certain things in the precise time of the teaching. Know, Nakala that all of our teachings encompass several 'players.'"

I had an acute sense that Babaró didn't really want me to know why he was choosing to direct me to do certain tasks or engage in particular activities. I asked, "How am I to learn if I do not really look at all sides of what is happening?"

"No, you misunderstand here." Babaró interjected. "It is expected that you ask questions but there are times when you must rise above in trust, indicatively, moving forward without all the hoopla that accompanies your string of judgments. You go into the scene and pick it apart to judge for yourself if this is for your highest good. I tell you, we know what is best for you. We see with expanded awareness what lessons are desirable for you at any given moment.

"Nakala, you still question. Take for instance your very physical existence may be threatened. Will you sit down and weigh the reasons why we direct you to get up and move before you are harmed?"

"Yes, Babaró I get your point but this past weekend I was given a day's notice that *maybe* I would be going to Medford."

"It makes no difference," Babaró countered. "There are times when we take you out of one situation into another simply because there are provocative reasons. It may be a matter of safety for your physical vehicle or perhaps a teaching on obeying our directives—to teach you that your suspicions and doubt vexes our relationship: this mistrust must be cleared entirely! The disbelief in our honor must be laid down and vanquished!"

Babaró continued, "As of late there have been several times when you have argued with our directives—saying you don't see the point in what we tell you to do or where you are to go. Miss this must end and it must end now."

I felt my heart sink and took a good, long, deep breath. Suddenly the memory flashed of my visit to Scotland. I had sat in the tour bus gathering my journal, water bottle, and rain jacket preparing for a hike to three different stone circles. I could see a path but mostly it was pasture with fences. I could see that I would have to dodge sheep poop and small areas of water. Soon I found the pasture to be more like a giant bog or marsh. Several times Nathanal had directed me to put my rain pants on before I left the bus. Each time I had asked, "What for? There is nary a cloud in the sky."

It had been a mere ten minutes later that I clearly understood Nathanal's instruction and shook my head in disbelief at my stupidity—my audacity at rejecting Nathanal's advice. The wind picked up in a matter of seconds and began to blow and the rain poured in torrents. Then the sleet had come in a horizontal wave. That lesson should have made its mark in a lasting way…yet it had not.

I knew that I had been argumentative in certain circumstances. It was a shame that my behavior had caused Babaró to feel he must correct me on it.

"Babaró," I am sorry, but I keep thinking of the first teachings Quem gave me. First: Honor the body as it is God's temple. It must get you through the physical walk on the Earth. Second: Listen to your heart. Do what makes it sing."

"Ah, yes. Nakala, dearest, part of why you were directed to leave your home—your area—was to get you out of the house—get some exercise, breathe some fresh air, stretch your perceived ideation that your physical body has these imagined limitations. I must conclude that sitting around all day is not conducive to a healthy body even if you are tired. The thing is you are tired because you have been in the house most of the week and not out in nature!

"I hear you ask, 'Well, why didn't you take me out in nature then?' We did…we took you for a ride through the mountains for over two hours. Given you did not walk on the soil through the trees but instead you looked at the trees, the sky, the mountains—all of that *blue, green, and brown* and all the shades therein! Wouldn't you agree that to be surrounded by nature is in itself a very healing experience? Indeed. Even though you were in your car most of the time you were very connected to nature. Your gratitude swelled beyond the ordinary capacity during nearly the entire length of the drive.

"To spend too much of your day indoors is not what we would consider a healthy balance. You are to make a concentrated effort to get outdoors every day and I mean for a longer period of time than it takes you to walk down the hill to retrieve your mail. Allowing the sun to shine on your skin and breathe the fresh air is most pleasurable and certainly to be taken as a gift! I go further: There are days a-plenty when the sun is hidden behind the stratosphere. When the cloudy days gather in sequential numbers, several, you will remember my words concerning this gift."

Just when I thought Babaró had concluded his teaching, I heard him say, "I go on to address Nathanal's reasons for having you look up the addresses to the before mentioned stores. Yes, we can tell you to turn right here and direct you to look at anything in particular. However, we felt it would be wiser to have you familiarize yourself with the layout of the city a bit better. When you went to each website there before you was a map showing you locations of the prominent stores or landmarks. This eases somewhat your constitution as you feel you have a better hold on where to go. Of course there was the issue of coupons. We simply are assisting you in saving a few dollars while we teach you the importance of balance.

"In addition, there is a matter of the directive that you were given: to pull-in your energy. You misunderstood just a bit the true meaning of our words. I clarify now. Yes, to have too many projects started is having your energy spread out too thin. As it is, your attention is divided—watered down. But the directive to pull-in your energy wasn't totally about your projects it was about your thoughts. Rein them in. Your concentration will increase dramatically. Much of what I speak of is on a subtle level as the thoughts are usually undetectable and seemingly hold little or no impact on your energy level. Quite the contrary, even subtle thoughts (thoughts you are not aware of) feed emotion and are extremely powerful. You are to be attentive of your energy always."

CHAPTER
TWENTY

A thud coming from the other side of the house had been loud enough to distract me from my writings with Babaró. It had been an unmistakable cause for concern. The sound wasn't the normal pop that I often hear when the guides want to elaborate on a statement or to call my attention to what I am thinking at the time. This time the sound had a different tone to it—an unexplainable solidity or heaviness to it. Either something had broken, fallen, or possibly one of the guides wanted to make a grand entrance for some reason. Anymore, this sort of thing usually doesn't startle me or even cause me to pause.

Even so, this time, I felt I should go see what had taken place. The sound came from the east side of the house. Because I was sitting in my office in the middle of the house, I had to walk through the living room and dining area. As I walked through the house I paid close attention to the energy. I scanned the rooms with my inner vision to see if I could detect any beings hanging around. Sometimes I will see them at the table reading or using these little devices that look to me like little hand-held computers or sitting on the floor somewhere immersed in some activity.

As I entered the dining room, I could sense three beings sitting around the oak dining table. Casually they lifted their heads and turned to my direction. Seemingly, uninterested with my presence they, returned to what they were doing.

There was nothing out of place. The plants were still on their stands—the curtains were still hung over the windows. Nothing seemed to have been moved.

Out loud, I asked, "Did someone want to speak to me or did someone just have difficulty getting through the wall?" Inwardly, I chuckled at my little joke. Then instantly I saw the projected image of Tulró momentarily holding the side of his head. The pieces were coming together as I watched Tulró duck under a crossbar in the wall that was now semi-transparent. (The outer and inner walls had been removed leaving the bare studs for me to see.) Tulró then lifted his floor-length robe high as if he were about to gingerly wade across a low-bed stream. All of his movements were highly exaggerated as he lifted his legs, one after another, as high as possible, to avoid contact with any of the joists. I saw his attention was divided as he kept shifting his eyes to see above his head, in front of his body and where he wanted to plant his feet.

He worked at his entry through the joists like he was climbing through some sort of elaborate maze. When Tulró had finally *arrived* he turned to face the wall and gave it a smug appraisal like no matter that you present yourself in a difficult manner *I will always* overcome!

With that, I announced, Tulró, "I'll be in the office if you want me for any reason."

I walked through the house having the feeling that Tulró was following me. The energy I felt was uncanny as I had never experienced this sort of thing before. Swiftly, I turned to look behind me to see if what I felt were correct and found myself nose to nose with Tulró. Startled, I gasped out loud and tried to get out of the way as Tulró was going full steam ahead. His eyes were focused on something beyond me. It was as if he didn't see me or perhaps couldn't see me.

I was well aware that Tulró was creating a pretense, (more like nonsense to me), as these guys are aware of where they are, what they are doing, and when to do anything, at all times.

Even though on a conscious level, I knew all these things, I had reacted: My heart pounded with fright of the near collision. Tulró, however, kept going. He walked through me like I wasn't there. I felt a swishing energy and was a bit uncomfortable as he passed through. After Tulró had made his pass, I involuntarily sighed. Noticeably, I was relieved on a not so subtle level.

I turned to find out where Tulró had gone and found him behind me waiting with his hands resting on his hips. Just as my eyes locked onto his face, Tulró screwed up his face with a half-cocked grin, threw his arms high in the air and sang in a high pitched voice, "Ta dah!" Tulró was treating the entire incident as if he had been on center stage. He had been preforming! Now, of all things he seemed to want to be recognized for his amazing feat. I had to agree, Tulró had a bit of talent.

Involuntarily, my hands moved to hold my head as I felt a pressure build akin to a headache. Even though I recognized Tulró's talent I was not at all amazed and felt a sense of disillusionment quickly beginning to blossom. Tulró was purposefully distracting me taking me from my writing. For that I did not appreciate his antics. "Tulró," I scolded, "You are not winning my favor by doing these types of tricks."

Then I realized Tulró had wanted to lighten my mood and I, without meaning to, asked in an accusing tone, "Are you here to teach or to play silly games?"

Tulró's face no longer eager to please, flatly stated, "Nakala, you, at times, are much too unyielding." Then he thrust out his lower lip and sulked like a young boy who had been badly mistreated.

Not giving in to Tulró's sad act I started in, "Tulró, contrary to what *you* believe, I have work to do. I had been writing with Babaró when I heard that bang. By the way, how do you do that anyway?" Tulró laughed then took my arm as he offered, "Here let me show you."

In a flash, I knew that the entire episode was one of his comedic acts geared to teach but in doing so he had indicated that he was about to *show* me how it was done. He was ready to take me to the wall and quite possibly would attempt to take me through it with him. He was that believable! I wanted nothing of it! Of course, I didn't have this ability to walk through walls, so my instinct was to be afraid and protect my body. Tulró's acting was so clever—so dead-pan that I almost had fallen for it!

In a swift jerk, I pulled my arm away from Tulró, took a step back and defiantly crossed my arms and planted my feet solidly on the floor in a protective stance. In a loud firm voice, I proclaimed, "Not this time honey. Ain't going do it!"

"Ah, Nakala," Tulró whined taking on that persona once again like an insolent little child that had been told it was time for his bath, "Like I said, you are way too serious. When are you going to lighten up and have some real fun? Walking through walls is the bomb!"

I just groaned and asked with words meaning to sting, "Why, oh, why won't you just grow up?"

Then I saw in a split second Tulró's expression shift from a happy go lucky young boy to an older man, his eyes sadly focused on nothing while he sifted through my words—my judgment of him! It seemed I had knocked the happiness right out of him. Before my very eyes, Tulró's had easily aged twenty years as the light in his eyes had dramatically dimmed changing from pure joy to utter defeat. I lowered my head ashamed to face him and I murmured under my breath but loud enough that Tulró could hear, "There is something seriously wrong with me that I would talk to you that way. I am so sorry."

Tulró had been, and obviously still was, one of my teachers. Why, oh, why was I having such a difficult time with him today? Why did I disrespect his jovial manner—his style? Disappointed with myself, I shook my head like I was symbolically shaking away the bad karma I had just created.

Wanting to avoid any more confrontations, I turned to seek the comfort of my emerald-green recliner. I sat down and buried my face in my hands.

At that moment, I saw an image of myself with an acute clarity and precision as if I had split into two people: the ugliness of what I had become, and asked myself, "Nakala, what have you done this time? How are you going to fix this?"

At once, I sat up with the knowing that Tulró had purposefully and shrewdly set me up. Once again I had been tested to see how well I could manage my thoughts and emotions—if I would act instead of reacting. In resignation, I sighed knowing full well that I would have the same test again and again until I had mastered patience, compassion, diplomacy, and a host of other virtues that ought to come naturally to me. Dang it! I loved Tulró. *Why did he have to be so completely annoying?*

Taking me by surprise, I heard Tulró politely ask, "May I speak?" Tulró had masterfully tipped the scale. I felt vulnerable, embarrassed, and guilty for my words and wasn't sure I wanted to continue the teaching, but I said, "Of course Tulró, you have my full attention."

Tulró channeled three breaths through me before he began to pull together what I would consider to be one of his finest teachings.

Tulró began by saying a single word that took me nowhere, "Stars." I shook my head knowing that we weren't finished by a long shot. Unintentionally, suspicious of his motive, I furrowed my forehead and wondered what on earth was he up to now? Tulró repeated the word, "Stars," once again, only this time I saw his expression and heard the tone of his voice like the word, "stars," was a code for some deep secret that only *I* had the key for—that *I* knew the meaning of. To my dismay, I did not know. I didn't have the foggiest notion of what Tulró was trying to relay to me here.

With a speed and accuracy that I have seldom witnessed with people on the Earth plane Tulró launched in, "Stars are beings that reside way up in your solar system, your galaxy, your universe. Wouldn't you agree?" Perplexed, I cautiously answered, "Well, it is said that stars are located in those places, yes."

"Would you say, Nakala, that stars are alive?" At that moment, I knew I had scrunched up my face working to figure out his riddle. At the same time my opinion was: his question was absurd, I mean really? But quickly I shifted keeping my opinion silent as I thought better of it. (All the while Tulró read my thoughts.) Still I had no idea how stars could possibly tie into Tulró's class act. Intentionally, I relaxed my face. However, still annoyed I managed to politely answer his question, "Yes, I do Tulró. I believe they are alive."

With my answer, Tulró gave me a single nod and exclaimed, "Well, there you have it!"

My mouth dropped open and I lifted my open hands toward the heavens in a receiving gesture but they remained empty just like my understanding of Tulró's lesson. "Oh, Lord," I prayed aloud, "Please teach me the ways of patience, kindness, understanding, and wisdom."

As if on cue, I could see an image of the beautiful night sky twinkling with too many stars to count. I stayed with the vision for some time and felt my vibration rise. The site was breathtaking—gorgeous! I felt a sense of peace—serenity.

To my surprise, Tulró broke the silence to whisper his child-like question, "What do you suppose they do up there, all the stars, that is?" Tulró had at last captured my full interest and appreciation and as if on cue I felt a reverence rise up in me before I whispered back, "I don't know Tulró. Look stunning, perhaps?"

As I spoke, I could clearly see in my mind's eye the images of the countless pioneers travelling across vast expanses of land and ocean who used the twinkling of the star-lit sky to illumine their way like a map or a navigational system. Then an image came to my mind of various vagabonds trekking through the mountains littered with obstacles like fallen trees, deep gullies and crevices and rocks of all sizes and shapes and across barren sand dunes during the night using nothing by the brilliance of the stars as a compass to get to their destination.

"Oh," Tulró said, as he swiftly swept his hand across my line of vision as if cleaning away my thoughts like a wizard would do with his magical wand. "The night sky has been used as a map for eons." Then added as if he, himself truly didn't know the answer, "but is that the true purpose of the stars?"

No longer did I want to get back to the book I was working on with Babaró earlier as I had become positively captivated by Tulró's story. I said, "You have me there." I felt an emotion well up in me akin to grief or despair almost as if I never fully appreciated the stars before this very moment and replied, "I do not know what their true purpose is…not really."

I heard the enthusiasm return to Tulró's voice as he readied himself for the next segment of his teaching, "Well, then, let me tell you." I saw him throw his head back as he took in an enormous gulp of air. Tears sprang to my eyes as I felt the power emanate from Tulró's small frame.

Love poured from him in such a way that I was overcome. I heard myself beg to Tulró, "Please stop." My emotion of gratitude and love was building, bringing in waves of tears that threatened to spiral out of control. Suddenly, I felt tired and wanted to compose myself. I remembered the book and Babaró, who was surely waiting for me to come back to him.

But nothing I thought or said convinced Tulró to stop. His face was animated as he put his hand to his heart and then to mine saying, "*We are all* grand expressions of Light. You see? Even the stars they are expressions of Light—God's Light—His Creation. The stars twinkle and shine. If you look upon the stars closely you will find that no two are alike just as no two people are alike. We all twinkle in our own distinct and utterly amazing style. This causes us to not only look but also behave in a unique way, Nakala."

As Tulró continued, I noticed his voice had changed taking on a deeper quality with an unmistakable edge that unmasked his authority, his wisdom, "I am quite capable of controlling my behavior." His voice became even stronger as he said, "My behavior is controlled! When I see a person or a situation that carries a lower vibration I like to bring forth the energy that brings on a smile or a laugh that perhaps will change the course of his day or even his life! I love myself. I not stop. This is who I am. Just as the stars that have been created to shine illuminating the night sky to guide those who walked the earth or those who navigated the oceans were created. They not stop. This is who they are."

"Nakala," Nathanal interrupted as he shifted his stance coming closer to me. Distinctly, I felt his energy as he moved in and put his arm around me and murmured, "Tulró is brother to us. As long as I remember he has been this way. We love him regardless. Tulró is grand Ascended Master. There is absolutely no one who has the skill to teach like him."

In my mind, I could see the two of them, Nathanal beside me and Tulró standing in front of me. The two of them had suddenly become quiet—stoic. There were no jokes, no laughter, nothing. The room had grown silent; no words were spoken. It was as if the light had dimmed somewhat in the room. I waited. Nothing came, so I said excuse me and went in the kitchen to heat up some lunch.

When I returned I thought about the stars shining so brilliantly in the sky, and asked Tulró, "What if their Light, for some reason, dimmed and they for some reason are no longer able to guide us as God intends?"

Tulró was by my side in an instant and said, "Exactly! What if for some reason the stars no longer were able to shine? They became dim and from the Earth couldn't be seen? What if the stars pulled back because a few people didn't appreciate them and felt their Light wasn't useful? Maybe the stars had been criticized or judged for some reason. Because of this they had gone into hiding: feeling that they weren't good enough—they were no longer beautiful—felt ashamed to be seen, no longer *wanted* to be seen and ultimately afraid to fulfill their purpose?"

It had become evident that Tulró was making a comparison between the stars and the people of the Earth. Or maybe it was him that he was making the comparison with.

I thought back to my childhood and the past lives I had knowledge of and remembered the times that I was so afraid and alone—the times when I had lost my life at the hand of another. There were so many times I held strong the emotions of fear, guilt, and shame. All because I had grown up believing these types of messages: You have fallen below the mark. You have done this or that against what society has deemed acceptable. Consequently, I grew up afraid to follow my heart's promptings: doing what made my heart sing! And I believed it all! Of course when your life is on the line you conform. Conformity will dim your Light that is for sure!

Therefore I didn't allow my Light to shine as brightly as I could have—not like God wanted anyway.

Tulró nodded once before he spoke again, "Nakala, dearest, you are a beautiful being who is learning to hold more Light—shine brighter; this is because you now hold the knowledge of who you are—you have the golden key."

CHAPTER
TWENTY-ONE

Suddenly, a palpable wave of energy descended upon me and I heard a voice that I did not recognize say, "You are keepers of the great Earth, Gaia; a bringer of a new day."

Beforehand, there had been no preemptive suggestion or meeting to announce the messages arrival or its ownership. With no other explanation, the message felt like it had plummeted down like a steely arrow that had been aimed and shot straight from the heavens in a direct fashion to make its mark exact.

I sat for several minutes with it, wondering if this were all to the message or if the speaker would so kindly entrust me with his name.

Taking a deep breath, I decided on another approach. I asked if the being who made that statement would reveal himself, please. I heard nothing. However, I felt my body stir and my vibration rise implying that someone had indeed gotten my request. Perhaps ownership, in this case, wasn't relevant.

As I considered the brief message spoken to me by the unseen, unnamed visitor, I felt a sense of failure and victory all in one sweeping gesture. The collective has taken advantage of this place, our Mother Earth that we call home using her resources without regard to her welfare. Many of us have hurt her—killed in her name for the perceived ownership of land, fame, and fortune. In the same token, many have been grateful for her gifts, loving her with all of their hearts and never taking more from her than they required for survival.

⁕ ⁕ ⁕

Just a few minutes earlier I had decided to take a rest from writing and walked down the hill to retrieve my mail. It is a lovely walk and just far enough to get invigorated for the next segment of writing.

As I walked down the street in the brisk air, I heard Babaró ask me if I were ready to get busy as the book could be completed in a couple of weeks. He went on to say that after the book was finished I could have a few days to myself and do something else I would enjoy.

My thought was, "I really didn't require…no, I didn't *want* any time off." But to see this book completed did sound wonderful. I could then move on to the next book.

A few weeks earlier there had been a clear indication to me that I would be moving in another direction, away from *The Accounts of a Pleiadian Traveler* series. The sound of doing something new did intrigue me somewhat.

Back at my computer I was ready to get back to the writing. From the previous conversation I fully expected to receive the dictation quickly. However, for some reason Babaró stood back as if waiting for something to happen. There are times that I wonder if I am being tested on patience. This is one of those times. Do I sit here and wait or should I get up and go take a nap or maybe just find something else to do?

Finally, I rose up to find a snack and get some more chamomile tea. It was then that I heard someone say, "Mikaelah, I am ready to begin." My heart stirred and I found myself grinning. Martin is the only one who calls me by that name. Perhaps this is why I had been waiting. I was truly happy to have him here.

"Nakala, I do know you by your given name—the name my brother Quem has bequeathed you. However, I prefer to call you Mikaelah, like a pet name. It is like a secret shared by the two of us, only. It presents a bit of joy when I call out the name Mikaelah, even though it is incorrect. I give it to you, Nakala. I am like grandfather doting on granddaughter-favorite." All I could do was smile. Martin has always shown affection to me and I had felt it on a genuine level.

"All in all," Martin began, "we are looking at the end of this series of books and going in another direction. It is time to try your hand at something new. Don't you think?"

"Well," I hesitated before speaking, "I have been having a great time writing this series, but yes, I would love to get the stories from the elders that have been promised to me. It seems like that book may be a bit of a challenge. But you know it really doesn't matter. I have come to realize that I will write what I am directed to write. I am sure that my I AM Presence knows exactly what would benefit me and our evolution for the highest good."

Martin shook his head knowingly in agreement as he said, "Yes, you are correct and you are always directed accordingly for the highest good."

"Let me say this, Nakala, you began the writings of another series called, *When Angels Speak: The Awakening, A Pleiadian Endeavor,* a few years ago. You were advised that there would be several in the series. However, you only were given one volume to have published. I'd like to explain what has occurred. The series has been laid down for a while. I believe, in time that the series will be picked up again. For now we concentrate on other projects.

"For you there have been many areas of learning in order to get the books in the hands of our dedicated students. It has been quite the journey. We are pleased that you stayed with the process.

"I say this, many imagine writing books, fewer begin to write books, even fewer complete the writing process and even fewer people than that get the books in printed form to be marketed and sold. You see many are not disciplined to carry forth this form of expression through to completion because they do not dream big! Fear is the principal factor. In the past, people unconsciously learned, or shall we say have been conditioned, to stay with what is comfortable.

"However, times have changed. Once again you are to believe in yourself and know your message (whatever it is) is worthy to be shared. You are to follow your heart's promptings to stay on the path.

"It is unfortunate that many do not realize their dreams on the lower level of existence—the physical plane. My words may seem conflicting but no matter how far along a person gets on the creative journey to complete their manuscript, energy is created and released into the cosmos to be joined with like energy. There is a grand pool of energy for the written works by authors. We rejoice!"

CHAPTER
TWENTY-TWO

I woke up with a bad headache and a stiff neck. As the day proceeded the pain increased traveling down my shoulders and back. Later still, I began to feel intense intermittent pain in my lower, outer calf. The pain came in sharp stabs that literally caused me to cry out. Seriously, I doubted if I would be able to tolerate the discomfort while I sat at my desk to write.

I have learned that talking about any physical ailment only creates more energy surrounding it, not only for me but for the mass consciousness—making illness stronger and more prevalent. Talking about it creates programs or belief systems that spread like wild-fire. One must be very careful to not take on energy or these belief patterns. So to sit here and write is causing me a little stress but I will press on as I have been guided to do this.

I dug into my mental tool bag of healing modalities to find the correct way to assist me to release the pain. I began by using fiats or commands. "This is not my energy. I AM calling forth my Beloved I AM Presence to transmute with the Sacred Violet Fire the dense energy back into its original pure essence: Light." I used a visual technique seeing the violet fire consuming all pain in my body. I then brought up love and gratitude with the pink and gold flames to assist in healing and sealing in the Perfection of the Divine.

I saw an improvement immediately. In addition, in order to continue at my desk, every few minutes, I would do neck rolls and other stretches to ease the pain which also somewhat relieved the discomfort. The thought of taking some pain relievers didn't ever enter my mind.

Unfortunately, the annoying soreness didn't leave entirely and at some points the pain shot through me like a sharp knife slicing deep into my muscles. Throughout the day, I repeated my commands, the imagery, and the feelings of love and gratitude. The pain continued to ebb and flow.

That night I had a meeting to attend. I weighed the pros and cons and decided because the discomfort had subsided to go ahead and go.

I felt that whatever I was experiencing had to be multi-level. Meaning there probably were several reasons for the pain and I should get to the root of the matter.

For months I had followed a strict diet to eliminate the over-growth of yeast, or what is called candida. My symptoms had improved yet if I slipped one time and consumed something that had sugar or that not nice product called corn syrup in it the candida would flare up with a vengeance.

Finally, I resigned. Two days ago I began a candida cleanse. I was told that during the detox I may feel like I had the flu complete with body and head pain. I thought I had slept wrong but as I write this I see that the culprit is probably the detox.

On the way home from my meeting, Nathanal said, "Take a couple of pain relievers. It is important that your muscles relax and you get a proper night's rest." Being in total agreement, I reached for my purse and found my emergency stash of pain relievers. Doing as he suggested, I popped in two pills and took a swig of cold water to wash them down.

In addition, Nathanal said, "Take a sea salt bath tomorrow night. This will assist tremendously. It is too late to do this tonight."

At this moment, I feel an overwhelming appreciation for my guides, especially Nathanal, and all they do for me.

In the background, I heard someone clear their throat like they wanted to speak but didn't want to interrupt my writing.

Suddenly, I was guided to look at the wood panel that is part of my desk behind my computer—specifically at the grain and saw a shape or pattern. The shape looked like a tuning fork. "Tuning forks?" "Yes, tuning forks," I heard, "Get yours out."

"Uh," I had to stop and think where I had put them. Instantly, I was telepathically shown the location of the tuning forks. I saw the closet and the purple storage box come into my mind, onto my "screen." I got up and found the box and rummaged through it finding the tuning forks down in the very bottom.

Not using the tuning forks all that often I reread the directions and followed them. During the session, I felt absolute peace. The pain had vanished and stayed gone for over an hour. Now, I just have the remains of a dull headache.

Nathanal added, "You are to go into the woods and breathe the fresh air, Nakala. Go visit the cedar tree behind your house and ask him to please assist him in your healing."

✳ ✳ ✳

Today, I woke feeling my emotions like they were heightened. During my prayers, tears had rolled down my face in streams wrecking my fresh make-up. No matter what I did the tears kept coming.

Nathanal reminded that this is part of the detox. The salt bath I had taken last night had assisted me greatly and I was to be consciously grateful for the release of the energy that was no longer serving me.

Yesterday, I had been sent up north to the next largest city, Yreka, to talk to an herbalist asking him if there were anything else that would benefit me to take during this cleanse besides the Pau D' Arco tea. The tea is highly beneficial in eradicating candida overgrowth. The herbalist had told me straight up that the tea wasn't the easiest thing to drink. I didn't care. I wanted this stuff gone!

While I was in Yreka Nathanal told me to drive to one of the grocery stores. As I walked by the grocery carts, Nathanal instructed that I get one. I didn't listen, reasoning that I rarely ever buy enough that I require a cart. Disregarding his directive, I made my way to the back of the store wondering why I was there. I saw the produce and began to formulate an idea that I was to check out the quality and to see if they had summer squash available. Then I saw the bins of squash and the price. They were marked at an all-time low for this part of California.

"Ah Nathanal, this is why you wanted me to get the cart." Nathanal simply shook his head, like you would make life a lot easier if you would just listen the first time. However, he refrained from saying anything.

Well, a little walking won't hurt, I told myself, as I returned to the front of the store to retrieve a cart.

After I was all finished shopping, I headed to the four-lane major thoroughfare and immediately had to slow down for a young doe who had decided to walk across the street. She seemed to be in no hurry or fearful of the on-coming traffic. She was beautiful.

After all of my errands were finished in Yreka I thought how odd to send me all this way to get one box of tea and a few squash. That is when Nathanal said, "We wanted to pick up Tulró." Surprised, I had asked, "Why do we need to pick him up when he could just teleport or get a shuttle."

"No," Nakala, Nathanal explained, "Tulró wanted to travel this way. He finds it more revealing on the condition of man. Call it an expedition if you will. He gleans information for later use." My reply had been, "Whatever we can do."

Unexpectedly, Tulró then announced, "Nakala, tomorrow we write together!" I began to push through a list of possible topics. I wanted to ask him if he would tell me more. Nathanal took over saying, "Not now. Tulró has gone into meditation."

During the drive home it was made evident that Tulró wasn't always the clown. He had a serious side to him. It was plain in that moment that he was here to serve God and in serving God he was serving humanity. I wondered what he did when he wasn't meditating, praying, or acting the clown. What sort of things did Tulró love to do just for the sheer pleasure of it? But of course, Tulró was not to be interrupted, not then anyway.

* * *

Today is the day that Tulró promised to write with me or as it is more accurately described: give me dictation. You must know that I am the scribe and I type what is channeled through me. I love what I do. I do use my voice to ask questions or in the dialogue we share.

Tulró was ready to begin, but instead of directing my thoughts to write he directed me to get up and go visit Trent the cedar tree.

The memory of Mother Sarah's advice to go hug Trent every day and ask for healing hung seemingly suspended in the ethers. I was also to give Trent the message that I was praying for all the Nature Elementals or Nature Spirits.

Without hesitating, I stood up and walked outdoors. Trent has a strong commanding presence and I held him like he was my closest friend. I gave him my message and asked him to please help me to heal. Trent said, "You must come visit me every day. Nakala, as you give so shall you receive. I speak of love." As I let go to return to my desk, I smelled the familiar scent of Jasmine wafting in the air. Odd…

Once back in my chair ready to receive, I heard Tulró declare, "Now, we begin. I have much to say. I have come forth today for reason special! One such reason is to inform the reader of the Pleiadian life-style. Ah, if it were as simple as that! The peoples who are from Pleiades are much like you of the Earth. We have our families and our unique interests as well. You remember, Nakala, that I love the flowers. I am besides ascended master one who loves to create anew—botanist. The Wisteria plant is my master piece, but one! The sweet scent brings pleasure to many.

"The Jasmine vine is another one that you enjoy as well. You have been gifted a plant that is stationed in your dining area—the Jasmine. You are to plant it outside this spring. As it grows strong it will give forth blooms a-plenty. What a pleasure to partake in its beauty that is given forth by its delicate lacy greenery of the vine and the tiny white trumpet-shaped blossoms. The scent of the Jasmine is to be enjoyed always!"

As Tulró spoke of planting the Jasmine outdoors, like a key that had unlocked a hidden passageway, I was reminded of yesterday's message from Saint Germain. He had said that I would be leaving this place to go on the road to market my books in two years' time. I had reacted to his words knowing that this day was to come, yet I didn't feel adequate to go on the road and market my books. Feelings of fatigue and fear began to rise and spill over. The thought of picking up again and going overtakes. I haven't recovered from the last move. From the sound of what Saint Germain said, it sounded like I would be selling my home and living on the road for some time. I would not have a home-base. I sighed at the thought of it all. On the flip side the travel would be exciting—a challenge.

Tulró channeled a deep breath through me. I shook my head and took another breath. Two years, Saint Germain had predicted, that isn't all that long of a time.

"Yes, Nakala, you will be fine." Tulró was speaking, his words firm and sincere. "You are to be ready to go forth into the world of form and present the gifts (the books) that have been bestowed upon you. Remember, one step at a time. Remember that each step is guided. All will flow easily, effortlessly."

Then suddenly the subject had shifted and so had Tulró's voice. "So this is what I have to say. Much of my time is in prayer. I visit the cathedrals, the mansions, the retreats as well as visit the areas of poverty. My prayers are for all!

"You remember my twin flame, Kasondra. She is member of the Telbar. We gather as often as possible. We both have assignments—areas of expertise. This is the way with most.

"You know, Nakala, we all enjoy life to the fullest. Our patience is without end."

At the mention of twin flames I thought of Nathanal and our way. I am in physical form and he isn't. To me it is difficult, yet easy. I am comfortable with him, even though at this time, I am unable to see him with my physical eyes. Although, there are times I am able to see him with my inner eye, it usually comes in snippets. I see his long dark-brown tresses, his muscular chest, his strong arms and lean legs. In my mind, I can and do touch him, kiss him—hold him. There are times when Nathanal will come and push my hair behind my ear with such tenderness just to let me know he is near. It is all done energetically. We have date night once a week. I tell Nathanal to send the others away. I want it to be just the two of us.

Then I ponder the fact that it would be nice to have a man in my life who would go to the theater, out for dinner, and do other things with me on a physical level. Sometimes it would be really nice to catch a break and have someone else take care of some of the things a home owner has to do. But really, I want someone to love who will love me back on all levels.

I have felt torn all along concerning this desire to have a physical relationship. Nathanal is always near me and assists me is so many ways. Yet, there is a part of me that feels like I am alone. I honestly don't know what to do—how to feel. I am told by my guides, even Nathanal, that a man will come my way to assist me as I finish up my lessons. In this life-cycle I am to have a partner in physical form. They say it is necessary. Then I look at all the women I know. There are so many who are single who are on the spiritual path!

"Nakala! Come back to me." Tulró commanded in a stern voice. "You have ventured far. The sadness overshadows just now."

Again, Tulró channeled several deep breaths through me and I began to feel lighter—freer.

"Listen," Tulró whispered to rouse my attention. Then I felt a surge of love wash through me and saw in my mind's eye Tulró bend down to give me a hug. Once again the tears spilled over. I felt drained. Again, I noticed the pain in my neck making itself known. "Nakala, I have words that will ease somewhat. Allow me to transfer the message." All I could say was, "Okay."

"There are beings, many, who hold you like babe. (Just then, the image of the cloud that had formed the shape of woman holding her baby in her arms came to my mind.) They protect and serve you as you plod through the teachings which incidentally include healing all bodies. There are to be days ahead, many, when you feel vulnerable. It is part of the coming of Christ. You are bursting forth, if you will, from an old paradigm. Because you have free-will you are accustomed to fighting and judging every new idea or concept—not allowing with grace the shifts to come. It takes moments, many, for you to integrate particular teachings.

"You are moving from one consciousness to a higher, or expanded, level of consciousness. With this move your heart opens into a state of *Oneness*. Instead of looking to serve your lower Self, you are seeking to serve all of God's creation.

"Nakala, you are in a transitory state now, thus you are in the midst of sheading layers upon layers of unwanted energy—old belief patterns and past hurts. Simultaneously, you are reprogramming yourself with new insights and feelings of authenticity! This transition is stirring the pot, so to speak. There are bound to be splashes of energy here and there that must be cleaned up.

"Now, as advisor and one of your esteemed team members, I would like to shift the conversation a bit. You remember the night of the coronation, when your father, Quem, and mother, Sarah, took the oath to uphold their nation to stand by the Laws of God to their truest abilities?" (Tulró was referring to the time Samuel Paul had assisted me in taking my etheric body to Mrya, Pleiades for a meeting with the Telbar. When I was there we signed a contract written by the Sirian Council of Light: Branch of Media Publications for a book contract. The coronation was to take place after the meeting. For some mysterious reason, I was not permitted to stay for the event. (The event was written about in *The Sacred Contract: Book II*.))

At first, I had been crushed (maybe that word is rather strong), that I wasn't there to see my Father and Mother crowned King and Queen. Now, I accept it but still feel like I missed out on a once-in-a-life-time event that was truly special; something that I should have been a part of. I worked to express my feelings on the matter gracefully saying, "Tulró, I wasn't there. I was politely whisked away before the ceremony."

"Ah, yes," Tulró responded as if he didn't remember.

Tulró tapped his finger on his pointed chin as if in deep thought. "As I recall, you were unavoidably transported back to your cabin in Prescott, Arizona. Am I correct that you were never told why you were brought back before the ceremony?"

By then I was rather annoyed with it all—our conversation, that is. He knew what had occurred and therefore my temper flared. "Come on, Tulró, you know the reasons were never explained to me. You have a mind like a steel trap."

Instead of checking myself, it was as if my thoughts and feelings had been unleashed like they had been held prisoner for ages. My voice took on a tone of superiority with a twinge of sarcasm indicating that I was someone of high of importance and had been set aside—forgotten or even abused. "Tulró, it was like I had been taken to this magical place that I was beginning to become accustomed to—familiar with. Then obtrusively, without cause or motive or even a tiny warning, I was bundled up and shipped home, away from it all! I was, without any consideration to my feelings even, harshly dumped back on Earth to a place—to a body that isn't all that great.

"I remember well, Tulró, I had been staying in Arizona. The entire trip I had been ill…too ill to write. I thought I may be dying. True! That trip was intended for me to get away and write a book. But, instead I had spent six weeks healing."

"Nakala, dear heart, listen. There is a lot here that you wish answered. Let's go back to my original question. 'Do you remember the night of the coronation?'"

"No, Tulró." Feeling more dejected than ever, I repeated, "I was not there."

"Oh, but you were. You have skipped over my question. You have translated it incorrectly because of a past disappointment. You were there that night just not at the coronation."

"Okay, yes, then. I was there. I am sorry. I heard what I wanted to hear."

"Yes, you did. You were prevented, for unjust causes, from attending that prized ceremony. You were hurt deeply, in fact. It is for this reason that I bring up the subject. Nakala, honey, the books are to be written in a certain sequence. The information is to be released in a specific fashion.

"Take the codes that were mentioned earlier. Nothing else has been said concerning them. This has all been preplanned."

"Okay, Tulró I get it. But why wasn't I able to attend the coronation? I mean, really? I should have been there for my parents and my family! I wanted to see my parents—the ceremony! I wanted to be a part of it all."

My emotions were full blown. I had erected a memorial of sorts that had been engraved with the words of betrayal, abandonment, resentment, grief, and anger then I saw in parentheses the phrase "Not Good Enough." I was shocked-flabbergasted at what I saw!

From Tulró I had expected to receive, in turn, empathy or at least a shred of some sort of an explanation so I delved in. "Now that you brought the subject up, Tulró, could you please just explain why I was brought back to the cabin just before the ceremony?"

Tulró's answer shocked me, "Not at this time, Nakala. I brought the subject up for another reason entirely." Devoid of emotion, Tulró informed me that we were finished for the day.

I looked at the clock. It read 4:15 PM. With a start I realized that I had sounded off without any reason. I did not have all of the facts. I shook my head thinking, "Way to go Nakala," and said, "Nice."

CHAPTER
TWENTY-THREE

Enough time had gone by that I was more than able to put two and two together. Tulró had provoked me—goaded me, even, into revealing my intimate and private feelings surrounding my trip to Myra.

For the last two years, my feelings had been firmly ensconced in the subconscious level of my mind—they were locked away in a seemingly impenetrable vault that only I had access to. Yes, I had the key, but had tucked it away safely out of sight.

Tulró knew that I had created those feelings and as one of the masters who assist me, he had used his expertise to bring it out of hiding—for me to begin the process of healing.

My travel to Myra, with the assistance of Samuel Paul, had occurred rather unexpectedly. I had not been given any prior knowledge that I would be going on this trip. As it were, my physical body had been put under, or into a deep sleep state, while my etheric body had traveled to the star system of Pleiades. This place is where the Akasie Family—my family, live. It is called the Kingdom of Myra.

My time in Myra had been exhilarating as I was at last with my Pleiadian family. Seeing the city and the sites had been spectacular and thought provoking.

I had wanted to stay in Myra as long as possible. I felt their love, but at the same time, during the meeting the members had conducted themselves in a respectful manner, even a business-like, almost aloof manner which prevented me from getting too enmeshed in my grief of wanting to return to my home. I hadn't known what to expect. Feeling somewhat uncertain of my role in that situation I had stood back, reserved a bit to observe the people: how they presented themselves. I remember those feelings, yet, I didn't consciously carry forward any of it into my present reality. It was all quite interesting as I had taken with me all of my memories of my life on Earth and my feelings of empowerment and inadequacies.

When I returned to Earth I was able to retain the memories associated with that journey enabling me to write about the episode with more than sufficient detail.

Unfortunately, when I was in Myra at the meeting, I had been afraid that I might let the project committee members—my family down somehow. I felt out of my element, like I stood outside the circle not really connected to the integral part of the group.

While during the visit I had flashes of memory (thoughts and even feelings) that Myra was my home, I had, in fact had, lost my memory of the place, its finery and the people. There was just a feeling that this was my home. During most of the experience I had felt out of place, like I didn't entirely belong. I suppose you could call the event similar to being reincarnated on Earth. There is a veil that keeps us from remembering what it is like in the Higher Realms. For most of us, our memories are wiped clean.

It may be equivalent to what an Alzheimer's patient may experience in the later stages of the disease, only in reverse. As an Alzheimer's patient proceeds through the stages of the disease he loses more and more of his memory until finally his memory is wiped clean.

Our meeting in Myra was held in the very same room as the banquet was to be held in directly following the coronation. I had seen the ballroom, the beauty therein. Some of the Pleiadians had come to the meeting dressed in full regalia. To me it had seemed obvious that there was something else that was to happen after the meeting, although I hadn't trusted the clues that had been given to me.

The marble tables had been elegantly decorated for the occasion. In my mind, I can still see thousands upon thousands of Wisteria blossoms that hung from the stone beams that formed the ceiling…I can still smell the sweet Wisteria fragrance.

That day, as a group, we had voted on the proposal submitted by the Sirian Council of Light to collaborate on a book project. The Telbar had recommended me to perform all duties associated with the position as scribe for the project.

Mother Sarah and Father Quem had both attended the meeting along with Quem's parents, who we lovingly refer to as Grandfather Adede and Grandmother Adrianna. Grandfather Adede and Grandmother Adrianna were officially stepping down that evening from the appointed positions of King and Queen of Myra.

The entire evening I had been in a quandary as how to present myself as I had never (on a lower conscious level) attended such a meeting and certainly didn't know the protocol. Part of me had felt hyper-vigilant—even fearful that I may do something inappropriate.

As I sifted through my thoughts and feelings surrounding this issue, I found myself wanting to get up and leave my desk (escape or run). I didn't want to explore any more of it. I wanted out. Babaró came to my side and gently stated, "Nakala, I am going to take over now. Tulró has another assignment to work on. Allow me to show you the way."

Feelings of embarrassment dominated but still there was a remnant of relief. I didn't need to think on his directive and gratefully replied, "Yes, I'd really appreciate your help with this, Babaró."

Babaró gave me a simple nod denoting his promise as he guided me to sit up straight. Then he channeled several breaths through me. At that moment, I felt the emotion well up from the depths of my being. Feeling out of sorts, I told Babaró that I wasn't sure about doing this because I felt this immense burden and I just didn't think I could hold back the tears much longer. In a very soft, assuring voice, Babaró instructed me, "Breathe through it. Allow it to dissipate. Call forth the

Sacred Fire to transmute the energy that holds you in bondage." After I did as Babaró directed, I felt the weight lift and the tears subside.

Babaró had stood by waiting for me to compose myself before he said, "Now, we begin. Yes?" I nodded, accepting his proposition.

"You know, Nakala, this subject that we have found ourselves immersed in is multifaceted."

"Of course," I replied, "Babaró, it always is. That is part of the reason that I didn't want to go on with it. It is so complex. I guess I am just a little tired."

As soon as I said the word, "tired" I knew that I had become unbalanced and heard Babaró ask (like he didn't know), "Nakala what did you have for lunch?" It was as if I had suddenly crossed some sort of invisible barrier. Suddenly, I remembered that I had neglected to eat a proper meal.

Babaró promptly directed me, "Go find yourself something nourishing to eat. I will be here when you return."

When I had returned, I did feel better and was ready to proceed with the writing. Although, when I had gone into the kitchen with my own thoughts away from the dictations, I had keenly recalled what I thought to be an error in the first book, *The Sacred Contract.* The meeting in Myra was conducted by the, *Telbar,* which is the group directly formulated to assist me with my ascension. It is the group, *Comterous,* who is dedicated to seeing to the publications of certain material in several areas of the media and literary fields. This is to assist in the evolution of mankind. There seemed to be a mix-up with the groups.

The revelation troubled me. I intended to take up the matter with Babaró as soon as I had gone back into the office and got comfortable in my seat.

"Yes, Nakala," Babaró said, "Much better. Please relax. I hear your concerns. I will address them shortly."

Babaró seemed at ease finding his focus as if he taught on this subject every day. "The scene in Myra, Pleiades, was written about in, *The Sacred Contract.* It for you, Nakala was very endearing because you had been escorted home in that scene. You were with your Pleiadian mother and father and much of the family. Nakala, for you, the longing to reunite with your family, us, on a conscious even tangible level, had been and continues to be so very great. So much so, in fact, that it brings forth pain in the physical heart emanating outward throughout the vehicle.

"It is understandable your feelings associated with this perceived decision or denial that you were not allowed to take part in such a historic event for the Pleiadian peoples. To be there just before the blessed coronation of your own mother and father and then to be suddenly whisked away for not one single good reason would seem to be a punishment of sorts. However, it was never intended to be thus.

"The intention behind all that we do is to break cycles or patterns that you have created through your many incarnations that do not serve you!

Bringing you back to Earth at that precise moment was used for this reason: To show you what it is like to be taken from something that is dear to you and that you love, and for the most part, your memory erased. Oh, no, not all had been wiped clear. There are still small but precious jewels left intact that keep you connected with your God Presence throughout your four lower bodies which are part of your Divine Cosmic Matrix. Your I AM Presence (Higher Self) has full record of all."

I thought I was beginning to understand where he was going with his discourse and asked, "This is about descending to Earth that first time and getting ensnared in the Earth cycles isn't it?" Babaró again gave me a slight nod before he answered, "Yes. When you came to Earth that first time, you came to assist others who had become trapped in the cycles. I compare it to be much like coming back to Earth just before the coronation. When you returned to Earth from Myra there was no memory of how you had traveled or why you had been expelled. However, there remains a deep feeling of rejection—separation associated with it all. You were simply dropped down—completely and irrevocably to the surface of the Earth. There was absolutely nothing that you could do to prevent or change your destination. Your desires were not granted.

There is a great yearning in your heart to return to the Pleiades, your home, not only but there is an unmistakable and immeasurable desire to have the full union with your family which can be taken symbolically as your deepest desire to return home to your God-Self: no longer do you wish to use the lower conscious mind to make decisions."

I wasn't paying close attention to his analogy but had instead become hung-up on my individual first-hand experience of being dismissed from Myra. "I don't get it Babaró. I had the memories of the meeting—the people—the place! But I do not have the memory of what happened just before I left. That was done intentionally?"

"Yes!"

Disbelieving what I just heard, I jerked my hands, like suddenly I was burned, from the keyboard and slowly sunk back into my chair and shook my head before I was able to formulate my words, "No! Why in heavens name would you do that to me?" Babaró answer was swift, "To reawaken, Nakala."

A shroud of sheer astonishment descended upon me like a large black cloud ready to let loose something very ugly.

Babaró didn't pause. "Nakala, I intend to explain this. But first let me answer your questions regarding why it was the Telbar instead of the Comterous who met in Myra and signed the contract with the Council of Sirius.

"Nakala, if you recall, during the meeting you had said that there was nothing more that would please you than to hold the position of scribe for the upcoming project but you were having a physical difficulty at the time and were unable to write. You were about to decline the offer when you stood before the group and made the declaration that you would agree to the contract if your body would receive the healing it required for you to go forward."

"Oh, yes, Babaró, I recall. I was a mess back then. I was left with nothing. At that point in my life I surrendered to God. I was ready to accept that quite possibly I would never write again and perhaps that was the last line of the road for me."

"That meeting was about your ascension, Nakala. It was about your standing up for what you believed in. That meeting was about your going forward with your Sacred Contract. Do you understand?"

I answered, "Not entirely."

Babaró paused for a few moments before resuming his explanation, "Yes, the contract was there to be signed. It was real. But it all hinged on if you were willing to step up to the plate and serve. Regardless, there was no error in which committee met that day, none whatsoever. Telbar is the committee formed for the purpose to see you through the ascension, yours!

"Now, I say to you this. The same scenario has occurred once again. You have found yourself suffering from candida. This has been known about for almost two years. The symptoms have manifested in your mouth and identified as Thrush. This medical issue is not all that uncommon, although it is not often talked of in social gatherings. We are grateful for that because the more illness is talked about the more momentum or energy is created for its existence!

"We choose to discuss it now as we are about to embark on the root issue for the disease. The mouth is associated with the throat chakra. It is about speaking your truth—to be in alignment with God. Your truth has always been to write the Divine messages in book format and get them to the masses. Always! However, there lies within you the emotion of fear that your work, even though it is transmitted straight from us, may be lacking in some manner."

Suddenly, Babaró shifted the topic. "It is exciting because there is a new group formulating in the Mt. Shasta area to bring together the authors of the area to represent their written works in an electronic form or catalog for marketing purposes! You, personally, have offered to assist wherever you are able.

"You have found clarity in your soul's purpose. You have stepped beyond the fear that held you prisoner. Fear is now a distant concept. There is joy once again. With this agreement there is peace; you are in alignment with your God-Self—your Beloved I AM Presence. All healing is to be completed. When you are in alignment with God your body vibrates at a higher octave. There will be no room for illness! Stay focused on loving life and all it entails. You are to *hold the vision* of perfect health and immortality."

CHAPTER

TWENTY-FOUR

Last week Sakeem announced that his Beloved Sebrina was finishing up her assignment and wanted to stay here at the house.

For some reason, I have interpreted it to be a hardship, of sorts, that the couples of the higher realms often work in different locations. This is my perception only. The thought that they would be reunited and finally have some time together gave me a sense of great joy.

Before I answered Sakeem, I wanted to clarify that the two of them would be comfortable in my home by asking Sakeem about it. (I still don't understand how the Beings of Light arrange themselves (living quarters). Sakeem assured me, "There is not a problem. We will work it all out."

"As long as everyone is fine with the arrangement and has a place of their own," I said.

For the entire time (about a year and a half) that Sakeem has lived with me I have known about Sebrina. During his time here there were a few occasions when Sakeem announced that he wanted to leave for a day or so. He would say, "Sebrina has a free day and I would like to spend it with her." To my knowledge, Sakeem has never stayed gone any longer than that.

Sebrina announced her arrival the next Thursday by coming straight to me and saying, "I come! I have been released from service earlier today. Happy." (Her way of speaking indicates that she doesn't use the English language much.)

With her arrival, I felt so much emotion that I began to cry, which, to me, seemed a bit strange.

Sebrina went on to say, "The tears you shed are my tears of joy! So happy to be here. Sakeem and I wish to take leave for a few days to see family and travel a bit. Thank you for agreeing to this arrangement and allowing Sakeem to move freely. Perhaps we will be gone for three to five days. We wish honeymoon of sorts."

Each day, after Sakeem and Sebrina's departure, I asked Nathanal, "Is Sakeem coming home today?" Each day, Nathanal answered, "We haven't heard from him."

I laughed as I said, "They must be having a really good time."

Sunday night, at the three-day mark, I repeated my question, "Nathanal, is Sakeem coming home tonight?" Nathanal hesitated a bit before he answered, "Sakeem asked for more time off." In a rush, as if I were in charge, I said, "Make sure he gets it!"

My words surprised me. Then I called on to Babaró saying, "You make sure Sakeem gets the time off he requires for him and Sebrina. When he comes home I want him to be truly rested and ready to return to his duties." In turn Babaró humbly answered, "Of course, Your Grace."

Being raised in a middle class family, I am not familiar with these idioms. First off, I was taken aback that I actually commanded Babaró to make sure that Sakeem got the time off. I have always felt that Babaró was my superior. After all, he is the teacher in this case! Secondly, this made the second time that one of my team members had referred to me as, "Your Grace."

Immediately, I went to google and did a search on this phrase, "Your Grace." I found it is a phrase or title representative of a particular social order or class. *Perhaps the title was used as a riddle or a clue of some sort?* The entire business baffled me. Why would Babaró talk to me in that style? I was still doing my Internet search when, suddenly, Babaró took my hand waving in front of the computer as if wiping away the computer screen, the information, including my search, evenly stating, "I take over."

The energy behind Babaró's movement felt off like he was upset somehow. *Do these guides get upset?*

A few moments later, Babaró repeated, "Yes, I take over. You are of the Royal Akasie Family. In that remarkable moment you allowed your true self—your true nature to shine through over-riding the lower consciousness—the physicality of this world as you gave the command for me to give Sakeem his leave. As heir to the throne, you had taken back your power—your authority—your rightful place in this family. For that I bow before you, Nakala, as I am but a servant placed before you to instruct and guide you through your training in this incarnation."

Babaró continued his disclosure, "Together we assist each other. Through our journey together, I am clearing karmic debt as well as preparing myself for another incarnation. To sum it up, I am in training, as well. We are both learning."

At that, I was promptly excused from writing any longer that evening as it was time to prepare dinner. Being more than ready, I saved and closed the file without delay.

However, as the night wore on, it became evident to me that something appeared to be troubling Babaró. I asked to speak to him in private and that we were not to be disturbed. I turned off the stove burners and sat down at the kitchen table giving him my full attention. I asked him, point blank, "Babaró, who am I to you?"

"Nakala, dearest, you are like daughter to me. As family member of the Akasie, I am very familiar with title and terms of respect. I say, 'Your Grace,' in honor of you. Nakala, you are in training to inherit the throne. You deserve respect!"

There it was again…to take or inherit the throne. *Is this an analogy of my preparation…the teachings that I receive in the ascension program?* All along I had suspected that perhaps these stories were nothing more than a way of conveying that I am going to the top joining with my I AM Presence, my Higher Self—that all is to become *One*—this is to attain the fifth dimensional consciousness.

Instead of voicing my suspicions though, I changed the subject asking, "Babaró what about you? Are you thinking of reincarnating again?" In truth, Babaró's answer startled and saddened me but also confirmed a dread in me that had been building. "Yes, I am and I believe that I am close to being ready, Nakala. I agreed to assist you with the writings taking you to a certain point. We are nearing that threshold. I have desire to search my heart—know the correct path."

With that last statement I felt he was attempting to gently guide me to accept his deviance from his position as my master teacher. However, something deep told me this was all a ploy to possibly gain my sympathies, or to put it bluntly, a bunch of hog-wash—a test to check my level of attachment, or neutrality, toward Babaró as my teacher.

"Babaró," I asked, "Don't you just *know* when it is time to move on?"

I detected a hint of sadness in his voice as he answered, "I know but I have an agreement. Nakala, please forgive."

I felt as if I had been knocked off-balance by his request, *Please forgive?* "Oh, Babaró, I love you. There is nothing to forgive. You do what feels correct for you. That is all I wish."

Babaró announced he was going for a walk, to be alone and think—to meditate.

A couple of hours later Babaró returned. Dinner had been prepared and eaten. The dishes were all washed and put away.

Often during these times of quiet I am able to piece together snippets of conversation I have with my guides and clearly recognize that they have cleverly inserted small but decipherable clues. To receive a full understanding one has to be cognizant that this is how the guides often work.

My thoughts lingered on Babaró's upcoming departure. I saw that several small pieces of the puzzle hadn't been placed together correctly. Babaró was easing me into this new idea. Babaró stepping down as my master teacher and head writer after all this time was sure a huge bite to swallow. If what Babaró said were true then there would be a replacement teacher selected soon, if not already.

Working to exchange data in a business-like fashion, I calmly asked Babaró, "What about the time frame of this alleged departure? Do you know when you would be leaving?"

His response brought up a keen awareness of my feelings toward him. I counted on him in so many areas, especially as a figure of authority. "Soon," he paused for added effect. "I will assist in the writings to finish this book completing the series of *The Accounts of a Pleiadian traveler.*"

"Babaró, we both know that this book is nearly complete. I somehow suspect there will be one more volume completing the series. Is this to be? What about the editing and marketing of the series?"

In a business-like manner he replied, "There is to be another who will assist in these areas."

With the conclusion of the conversation, it was becoming apparent that Babaró had thought through this scheme for some time and had already made some, if not all, of the steps to finalize the transition taking him to the final stages of withdrawing. The finality of his decision had made its appointed mark. However, I controlled my voice—no emotion betrayed, and I stated, "So you have applied to the Board to reincarnate then."

"Yes," was all that Babaró offered.

Wishing to be supportive of Babaró's decision, with enthusiasm, I said, "You will be accepted. I am sure." Then it hit me. Babaró had already been approved. He just had to finish up some details and then he would be leaving his post.

Is this all a fluke? It was precisely three days past that I had openly acknowledged to my guides that maybe it was time to move on myself concerning the books—work on a different style or level of information. I have thoroughly enjoyed writing the series of *The Accounts of a Pleiadian Traveler* but perhaps I could better serve humanity by writing material on a more expanded level. I added that I will serve wherever is for the highest good. I saw Babaró's full frame with his beautiful shoulder-length white hair and beard approach my side and place his hand on my shoulder. "Nakala, honey, you know there are no coincidences."

CHAPTER
TWENTY-FIVE

As of late, I have incorporated, with more persistence, the practices of going to visit the tree I call Trent each morning. The hugs are, for me, a way to get outside and drink in some fresh air, ground myself, release any dense energy and expand my love.

One of the main reasons, I felt I was being drawn to move to California was to serve to bring in the rain. On a personal note, I wanted to get to know the beings that makeup the Nature Kingdom. I felt my purpose was to assist in the balancing of nature which includes balancing the climate. However, to truly assist, I required the correct knowledge to bring forth the proper amounts of rain to different regions.

Throughout my household relocations in Kansas I had just started to practice connecting to the spirits of the air (sylphs), using affirmations to attract the spirits that brought rain. I called them the cloud or rain people.

On a few occasions when I had gone outdoors and began to talk to them, I had seen the clouds appear, gather force, and multiply before my eyes—even giving forth a light sprinkle when before there hadn't been a single cloud in the sky. This activity had brought me such delight, even though, my conversation (prayer of gratitude) seemed to be one sided—me doing the talking as I never heard any of them speak back. I understood they were responding but I had wanted a conversation of sorts. I felt though, it was only a matter of time.

Unfortunately, at the time, I hadn't yet developed a significant dedication to my practice to the point that I was able to make a real difference, and bring in substantial rainfall. Nevertheless, I felt, and still do, a strong desire to show these beings that they are loved and appreciated.

I have lived in California now for five months and even though I don't see the rain, every day, I have made it part of my daily ritual to give thanks for it. Somewhere it is raining.

It has been several weeks since our last rainfall. That last thrust of energy was substantial but still yet we require much more to get caught up and prepare us for what will be required in the coming months to not only grow our crops but to live in abundance in all areas. Water is Life.

Last week, I felt something should be done. This area was still severely in drought. I contemplated what I should do. I purchased a book that Ted Andrews had written entitled, *Enchantment of the Faerie Realm.* Even though the book is a little older, displaying a copyright date of 1993, it is chock-full of useful information. Ted is also the author of *Animal Speak* that is immensely popular in many circles.

When I purchased Ted's book, I held the intention that I would delve into and study it in fullness; to groom me for the connection that I sought—that I may call upon the appropriate Nature Spirits and Elementals for the supply of rain and more specifically to aid in the stabilization of nature during the shifts.

Even so, I felt I couldn't delve into the reading of the Faerie book because I was immersed in the reading of Paramahansa Yogananda's book, *Autobiography of a Yogi.* One of my rules is to finish one book before beginning another. So the Faerie book lies in wait.

The more days that passed before I did anything concerning the rainfall, the stronger this sense of urgency grew, with a perpetual cloud of energy overhead and with the unmistakable message that it is time to begin my communications with the Nature Kingdom! It was as if this energy had taken on a presence of its own to the degree that I was almost obsessing over it. I felt that I was to do something—*had* to do something. Our country requires people who are dedicated to *holding the vision* of balance, harmony and peace—Heaven on Earth.

Because I didn't know who else to turn to, I turned to Trent. I had stepped off the back porch a few feet to give Trent a loving hug. I held him tight feeling the energy flow between us directly through my heart before I asked, "How do I go about bringing rain to the area so everyone may thrive?"

Trent had paused a few moments before he answered, "Let me talk to some of my friends to see what can be done." He then added, "Please remember us in your prayers."

Before I released Trent from my embrace, I heard someone recite the following poem.

Thank you Lord
For the beautiful trees.
They stand proud and strong for Thee
Always with the desire to please.

They are a mantle of Love
Manifest in physical form
Given to man
On his earthly sojourn.

Thinking that Trent meant he would gather with his "buddies" and figure out something, I let it go with the intent that in the next few days Trent would have some sort of clear directions for me on how I was to proceed.

The next morning, though, I woke up to overcast skies and the temperature had noticeably dropped. I went outdoors to thank Trent. He said, "I have not completed." But to me it didn't matter because it was obvious that the energy was shifting. For that I was most grateful.

Trent said, "The rains come." Indeed they did!

Today, again, I went outdoors to connect with Trent. In doing so he said, "Go inside and get your book. I wish to give message." I was really surprised that Trent would instruct me to get my journal. How did

Trent know that I wrote? I asked, "How do I do this? Do I bring the book out here and sit while you talk to me?"

"No, you are to receive inside your home where you will be comfortable and warm."

My thoughts advanced from what I had known previously to the possibility of telepathic communications with Trent while I was physically in another place: I wasn't required to hug Trent or be in his presence in order to receive his insights!

Even though this had become evident, I continued to be counseled to visit Trent every day in reciprocation of energy. I was to continue to accept support from Trent as I was to lift up the Nature Kingdom through Trent.

This is what Trent said:

> I desire, as counterpart and co-creator, to assist you, beloved Nakala, on your quest to connect <u>with</u> the nature dévas and elementals. To achieve oneness with nature! It is in your DNA (heart) to bring forth harmony to this great Earth, Gaia. There are others, many, who desire to assist in the calming of the Earth shifts—to put forth the energy required to ease and balance all. It takes many such as you to create harmony.
>
> You, Nakala, have openly asked how you may connect with sect (dévas, elementals and so on), who make up the Nature Kingdom. I say for now, come to me, speak your desires to me as I am connected to all. In time your energy will be accepted and honored in all locations—forever!
>
> You have grown the love (allowed yourself to reconnect with heart) and go forth giving of yourself to this kingdom, not only, but to all kingdoms that make whole this place.
>
> Bring to me your desires.

After Trent had finished his message, I asked for cycles, two inches of rainfall per week until the reservoirs were full. After the bodies of water were full then the rainfall was to be adjusted to keep them full.

That night I awoke to the sound of rain hitting my roof and the ping-ping of the water making its way down the gutter downspout. I laid awake for some time before my excitement leveled off enough for me to return to sleep. The rain continued for one day.

*　*　*

Yesterday was my day off from writing. Even though the temperature was in the low sixties, I was instructed to go purchase the items (groceries) to carry me through for the coming week. Trent, along with my guides had given me fair warning, "The rain comes! The snow comes! We want you home with enough fresh produce for several days." Later in the day the wind picked up and the sky clouded over. I knew then that someone meant business.

Again, I awoke early this morning to the sounds of rain falling on my roof-top lasting well into the day. Later in the day the wind calmed down and I thought that was it for this round. No, I was guaranteed, another round comes within the hour. A few moments later, once again, the wind picked up with tremendous force. I do believe writing about this is encouraging someone.

CHAPTER
TWENTY-SIX

As it happened, Sakeem and Sebrina took a full five days for their holiday.

Sakeem didn't announce his return. Wednesday morning I noticed that the guide who was speaking to me had a more pronounced accent. I finally asked, "Who is working with me?" My question was answered quickly, "It is I, Sakeem."

Not trying to hold back my excitement I stated the obvious, "Your back home!" Sakeem had been away long enough for me to stop asking for him and for me to finally accept his absence. Now, here he was!

Wanting to know all about his trip I didn't hesitate to ask, "How was your trip?" Noticeably Sakeem was overcome by emotion as he was anxious to convey his good time. He stuttered a bit as he repeated how wonderful his trip had been.

Then I asked about Sebrina. Sakeem, volunteered that Sebrina had had a wonderful time as well and was resting. Sakeem continued to talk a bit faster than usual and added, "Sebrina told me to GO and let her rest!" His delivery of Sebrina's admonishment was so funny that I burst out laughing. The flip side, his interpretation of her rebuke, had sounded so much like something I may say it was uncanny.

My imagination whirled. Why did Sakeem begin to work directly without announcing himself first? Why didn't Sakeem want to rest as well? Maybe he was just joking with me. It was all too funny that Sebrina would want Sakeem to just leave her alone! No answers were offered as I turned to continue my task at hand.

"Miss," Babaró broke the silence. "We all require time alone to rest which is a restorative process. We also are compelled to retreat for a time to think, pray, meditate, and to imagine!"

"There are times that we, as your guides instinctively know when it is best for you to take time for yourself—to go into silence. We step back and allow you this. It is necessary for development—to evolve."

With Babaró's comment I had retreated back in time to the first times I had been left in silence and commented, "Yes, there are days that I have noticed that my team will be very quiet. If I ask a question I would be given a curt answer but would not be further engaged in conversation. At first, I hadn't understood why no one would talk to me! Now, I have grown to appreciate that you give me this gift of complete silence."

✳ ✳ ✳

The rain began just as Trent had predicted and it continues. I am mesmerized as I watch the wind blow the trees several feet in any given direction. (Some of the trees easily reach the heights of seventy to one-hundred feet tall.) With the interplay of the wind and rain the bulk of the trees swayed and the foliage danced as if they are immersed in an intricate and intimate ritual that only nature may take part in.

Full of joy and gratitude that Trent and his friends had somehow brought the rain, I went to the back door and telepathically said, "Trent…you guys…" I wasn't able to complete my sentence as my appreciation was so high. I was laughing just like a young child would at the scene before me. Trent beckoned me, "Come play!" I knew then that the beings were in celebration as the wind and the rains were integral parts in a fantastic rhythm that they had created.

Being from Kansas, for me, to see these gigantic trees lean from one side to the other with such agility was an awesome experience. Earlier, I had gone to the window to see if I could see Mt. Shasta. Of course, on rainy days the mountain is in enveloped in fog—a swirling shroud of mystery. As I gazed outdoors, my attention was drawn to the ground. I noticed that the rain had formed several small streams flowing downhill toward the creek that was no longer a peaceful bubbling brook but now was a muddy torrent. The land had had its fill. Several small ponds had begun to sprout growing ever wider and deeper. A twinge of nervousness made itself known in the pit of my stomach.

My concern was as long as I stay in this state of gratitude the rain probably won't stop. *What should I do?*

Once again, I went to the back door and looked out the window at Trent. I wanted to ask Trent if I should tell the Nature Spirits and Elementals that we have had enough rain. I called for Trent. As soon as I said his name, I heard, "Let them have their fun."

"What do you mean, 'let them have their fun?' Who is speaking?"

"It is I, Trent. You have called on the Nature Spirits and Elementals to bring forth goodness to the Earth and all life forms. For the Nature Spirits to be acknowledged as the keepers of the rhythms of nature is to respect them. It is a joy for them to serve in this manner. I say, you should see the little people (faeries) dance in the rain. This for them is a time of celebration *fun!*"

Having never seen a faerie in real life, but only renditions of them in various books and movies, I felt that I couldn't truly imagine what they might be doing. Perhaps they sat crouched under mushrooms or in rocky crevices to keep dry. But that wasn't the image that came. I clearly saw a little person with slight build and curly blond hair wearing her rain garments—her shining lime-green slicker, umbrella, and goulashes! As I sat with the image, I could plainly see her, like a child, splashing in the puddles of water. She was having such a good time of it.

"Yes," I agreed, "let them have their fun."

Sunday came and the rain continued. I didn't care as I had planned to stay home and work on my crazy quilt.

Later in the day the rain let up, turning to a drizzle. Finally the rain stopped altogether and the skies returned once again to a beautiful azure blue. Thank you, Nature Spirits and Elementals for your gifts!

CHAPTER
TWENTY-SEVEN

It had become expected—habit. Every Sunday morning at 9:00 AM I was to be ready for my Mother Sarah and Father Quem. Before their arrival I prepared my home by lighting white candles, placing certain crystals on the altar and playing some angelic music. Then I would sit for a few minutes in silence and meditate.

We would pray together and then I would receive a teaching from them. I felt blessed to share this time with them. For me it was a very sacred time that we shared.

However, after a few months passed with this ritual, something new and unexpected happened.

Before I go forward with the story I must backtrack a few months. This shift occurred before I had prepared my home in Kansas to be sold and my move to California.

As usual, on Sunday, I prepared the space and sat down to receive my Pleiadian parents, Sarah and Quem. There wasn't any inclination that this meeting would be any different.

When Mother Sarah and Father Quem arrived, I was directed to get a new journal and write the name, *The Pleiadian Council of Light* on the cover. Quem began the meeting, like usual, with a prayer. (I wasn't able to record the entire prayer.)

TRANSMISSION ONE

We come together today in reverence to our Father-Mother-Creator who reigns over all in the name of Christ. Amen

We see much has been accomplished in this home and we are pleased to give forth the release of your presence here (Shawnee, Kansas) as your contract has been met in entirety.

The energies that you feel bubble up of sadness, anger, and grief are to release you from your past ties—to these people, your energetic qualifications and endeavors. It is time for you to move on to another experience—journey. All is well.

These feeling—energies are to be expected and you are to relax in the knowing they are to assist you in moving forward. You are letting go of energies unwanted—unneeded. They bind you—control you. All is to be transmuted into LIGHT!

Dear daughter, Nakala, all is well within the Realms of Light—those who watch over you—assisting you in all steps on the Earth plane.

Currently, you are heavily burdened with several works. It is time to complete and let go of the energy. Finish the first book in the series of *The Accounts of a Pleiadian Traveler*. It is a joy to see you love the writing as you do.

Remember, Love, all works serve particular and we give unto you these written works for the highest good.

Our numbers are many. I am your Father, Quem. I am a member of this council.

Torah Tee sits at the head seat on the council. He came to you a few days past.

Torah Tee is ready to see you in your rightful place as we are all one!

You asked if there were a window when you are to travel—a specific time to be in Mt. Shasta—if you were to leave behind belongings. Perhaps, you asked if you should return at a later date to retrieve them. The answer is yes, there is a window.

The end of June we travel. Contact Joe and find out his plans. [Joe was one of the four of us who had traveled to Mt. Shasta in

February and heard the call to move there. At that time of my call he was not ready to make the move.]

We see the house transferred to new ownership by June 15— Father's Day. We work to sell your furniture before you leave. [I actually walked out of the Shawnee home for the last time June 14.]

Journey new. Contract new. As of yet, you do not know the true purpose of your new contract. All is unfolding.

You will continue your channeling, writing, and teaching. In addition, there is more. You are to bring forth the Lemurian teachings to the forefront. There are others who have begun this work. You are one who will assist in the continuance of the connection between the Peoples of Telos and those who reside on the surface of the Earth. Do not misunderstand it takes many to establish. You are but one.

You are to join with many—connecting to establish sector or area of expertise expanding knowledge that will serve to bring together all. You began this work long ago, Miss. Once again, it is time to serve in this area. We are with you always. Always!

Five months later the next transmission had been given after I had established myself in my new home in Weed, California. (Weed is fifteen minutes north of the city Mt. Shasta.)

TRANSMISSION TWO

Quem gave thanks before the meeting. (I did not document this as I was in prayer as well.)

Babaró spoke: Today is Sunday. The Flame of Illumination is greatly amplified. We are sending our thoughts and prayers that this great yellow flame is amplified and easily felt, seen, and heard over the entire planet. All is being illumined—such beauty to behold.

Tiger Eye and Topaz are the stones that support the Illumination Flame.

Nakala, thank you for preparing this home for the council's meeting this morning.

To begin with, for your benefit, Nakala, we will announce the presence of all who are in attendance today: Quem, Sarah, Nathanal, Babaró, Suzette, Samuel Paul, Nakala, Sakeem, Jonson, Tabitha, Camille, Tulró, Ahseem, Napoleon, and Christian. There are others who are viewing the meeting remotely adding to the amplification of intention.

New names, new faces—not all are members of this council. However, we have invited many, as these people also assist to amplify our intentions are those that have been created long ago and those that are created anew; all intentions that are held in this moment.

We have special for you, Nakala on this day. You are princess of Myra. Princess Nakala [I saw in my mind's eye all bowed before me.] I said, "Thank you."

You have not really seen yourself in this light because of the life you have lived on the Earth. But truly this is who you are. We bow to you and your courage to embody at this time in this realm. Indeed a sacrifice.

Together we could be enjoying the luxuries of Myra right now. Instead, we plot our strategies—our next move to assist those who reside in the lowers spheres of Earth in spirit and physical form. I speak not only of those who have passed on but also those who reside in the human form and all those who are members of the Elemental Kingdoms as well. All must be emancipated from the effluvia. You must all go into the beautiful Light.

The first and only meeting you have been privy to was before your move from Shawnee, Kansas. We were much in celebration with the plans to come here to California and begin our celebration in this energy near the great sacred mountain of Shasta and his glorious counterpart, Shastina. They hold and balance—the energy in this area. Yes, a great vortex has been established here amplifying all energy, be it positive or negative, it matters not. It is best, Nakala, to set your intent knowingly.

It is a true honor to BE in celebration here! The view alone of the glorious mountains lifts up high the emotions of love and gratitude.

We are pleased you have settled here. There are no expectations to send you off to live in another land or another home. You are here for a time. Yes, much energy was used moving you—the objective had been to get here. All!

Every shift, be it mental, emotional, etheric, or physical, has been in part, for preparation to come and live here in this grand place to experience this grand adventure. [This reference was to the four physical moves to different locations in the last two and a half years.]

Now, the reason for our meeting is to plan our next step to bringing forth the project—the books, all, into the hands of the readers. We came together this morning to share with you that all who have gathered here or be it remotely are in a sacred space amplifying the intention and *holding the vision* that the books are written perfectly and in a timely manner. They are then dispensed to the masses accordingly for the highest good. All!

We know this project is dear to your heart and we know you require push…guidance in order to continue forth. Always know we are behind you supporting this endeavor.

The Pleiadian Council of Light is involved in many projects. This one, yours, is but one. Nevertheless, it gets our attention, full!

You are one of the trusted and valued scribes for the Pleiadian Nation. We thank you. Because you believe high that this is your true and sacred path beauty, abundance, and grace, will continue to flow through you into the writings easily like the bubbling brook waters down the mountain slopes revivifying all that is in line with its course. Like the stream, as you travel, you are effortlessly expanding ever outward as you extend your electronic force for all to benefit from.

Don't become too comfortable as we must continue to go forth into territories unknown to further open the heart, expand awareness, and consciousness to further raise your vibration. The goal here is for you to reach full momentum attaining the fifth dimensional level of consciousness.

We back you 100% with your partnership with Adama. Sakeem is here to attest to this. He, Sakeem, is to continue his support until the contract has been met measure by measure in fullness.

Sakeem's dedication to you and the Lemurian's cause [the specific sector of Telos] is strong—never wavering.

Tabitha and Jonson are also here to assist with the Lemurian's disclosure as there are others who have joined with people such as you to assist in the endeavor. The time approaches when all are to be united as *One.*

The message here is: You have our full support and attention. You will continue on like you have. However, it is time and expected that you connect with our energy on more expanded level—even more committed than in the past making this endeavor invincible! There is no stopping us!

Yes, you have free-will and should you desire to remove self for any reason, we shall not bind you. However, we know your honor, loyalty, discipline, and LOVE for the peoples.

It is time we close for today. It is important to gather like this—regroup—reset our intentions. We are pleased to have these moments. *~ We are One~*

TRANSMISSION THREE

~ We are One~

We begin today in remembrance of all those who came before us to illuminate our paths preparing us so we too may tread in *Light* instead of darkness.

You were directed, oh, yes, to a spiritual teacher who lives in the area. This direction was for purpose to bring together group significant. This teacher receives the guidance accordingly. It is time.

Masters you all are! The lives you have lived together? No, on this level your memory sleeps.

Last eve, you felt the affinity—the suggestion of friends of long ago who had at last reunited once again. Did you not? There were no airs put on—all, as you put it, was REAL.

There was representative in attendance for The Pleiadian Council of Light at the event in addition to representatives for other councils as well. Rooms were overflowing!

You ask my name. I give you, Jordan. I am council advisor. We work to bring together certain who have taken embodiment in order to shift out of the old into the new! I speak of the Unification of Consciousness.

This is your reality and you must create anew! This is one of the universal laws. We assist, gladly!

A group has been established that forms your committee. You have entwined yourself with the energies of this group, creating *One*!

Make no mistake of what we say here and now. The members of your committee are totally committed and you have already begun the shift. Continue on!

* * *

Now, concerning the books written by the Comterous: you are being given special.

Samuel Paul has received new book for you to write. The other is to be disregarded. You begin tomorrow. It—the transmission, will go quickly. For you, create and amplify Love, confidence, and gratitude. This is required in order to carry endeavor forward.

The book you previously worked on, *In the Light of Day*, was used for healing purposes. However, some of the text will be used in the coming book. You will soon write the conclusion to bring readers into alignment with coming volume. In other words we make some adjustments with writings.

The series has been completed in the higher realms and will be handed off to you quickly, Nakala. No more delays.

This particular meeting began early. Learn to be flexible with meetings—all communications. What we do here takes precedence over all. Balance is key.

[At that point I was wondering why the council was giving me directives concerning the project.]

Comterous is a branch of the Pleiadian Council of Light. There are many branches or affiliates.

Your mate (husband) is being brought in now. Balance regarding that matter is of utmost import.

Remember each morning to ask for Divine guidance and how you are to serve.

We oversee your activities. We signed off, or offered up our agreement, shall we say in revealing the following book(s) at appropriate time. Not only for you but for others who walk the spiritual path of Divine Light.

Might we add we are pleased with the changes you have made with All! Incorporating new ideas to expand this is essential. Go forth my child. Today is a special day. *~In Love~*

Those in attendance: Jordan, Alexander, Chameece, Tulró, Nathanal, Daren, Careece, Samuel Paul, Sakeem, Benjamin, Stephanó, Jonson.

The people listed are not necessarily members of the committee (council) but are members of other groups directly connected with your work and healing. *~We are One~*

＊ ＊ ＊

Throughout the writing of this book I have been reminded again and again to *hold the vision*: I am a mirror for others. I am to hold the Light so others may see the Light in themselves!

But this isn't the entire teaching. I am to continue to *hold the vision* to manifest goodness and create Heaven on Earth. In order to create Heaven on Earth we must *all hold this vision*. As custodians of this Earth and co-creators of the third dimension (now shifting to the fourth and fifth dimensions), we use positive intentions to create our experience: no one will do this for us and no one can do this for us!

To manifest a specific creation we *hold the vision* of what we want (or don't want as this works both ways) as an individual and or a collective consciousness. This is done with both positive and negative thoughts. (Up to this point I believe as a collective we have been manifesting more with negative thoughts than positive.) There is power in our thoughts that is fueled by our emotions. The challenge is to stay focused on the positive in all situations and things—look for the good in all people!

CHAPTER
TWENTY-EIGHT

When I first arrived in Mt. Shasta, I checked into a small but accommodating motel on the main thoroughfare. While I stayed there, I passed my time by looking for permanent housing, writing, making trips to the Mt. Shasta City Park to fill up water bottles with the Sacramento Head Waters and going to different shops. On the weekends I would pick up a local free paper and scour the garage sales. This helped me in learning the streets of Mt. Shasta as well as getting out and socializing a bit.

One particular Saturday, Nathanal guided me to go to a yard sale just north of the city. I drove to the site, pulled over to the side of the road, all the while wondering why I was there.

At first glance, there was nothing there to look at that I thought was even worth getting out of the car for. Nevertheless, Nathanal told me to park Sarah Jane Blue and go have a look.

I did as directed and walked up to tables overflowing with stacks of used books. (Just so you know books were something I had no desire in purchasing.) Working to figure out why I had been sent there, I busied myself perusing several books. I had no idea what I was to see or hear so I just stood there and waited. Out in the parking lot there stood three men who were engaged in a heated discussion. I noticed that a very quiet woman sat in a lawn chair near the tables that displayed the books.

Immediately, I assessed that the large assortment of books were meta-physical, which is nothing unusual for Mt. Shasta. I busied myself by reading the various titles and book jackets to see if any interested me. I kept thinking that there had to be a book here that Nathanal thought I'd like.

The conversation between the men continued. The longer I stood there and listened the more I wanted to engage myself in the conversation as I was very interested in the topic the men were discussing.

As I recall, they were talking about the city's water and a particular water bottling company that was preparing to set up shop in the area. There was already a large manufacturing plant that was available for them to move into.

These men were against the water bottling company's proposal. The issue: this company was deep into moving its production to Mt. Shasta and wanted to bottle free spring water (the cities and surrounding area's resource) to sell. In addition, they would be using plastic bottles. (Plastic has gained notoriety from environmentalists as a hazard for our Earth, animal, and marine life.) The men went on to speculate that the heavy equipment (trucks) associated with the company would most assuredly congest the city's traffic and be a problem especially during tourist season.

Finally, one of the men noticed that I was listening in and approached me. He glanced at the book I held in my hands and asked, "Do you want to buy the book?" My response was, "How much?" He tilted his head to the side and then answered, "Ten cents. We like to just pass on books."

The man added, "If you want it you should get the companion book. I edited it. My name is Carl."

I worked to stay centered at the information that had been suddenly and without any provocation dropped into my lap. Trying to act neutral until I had more information, I responded, "Oh, I see."

As I began to piece together why I had been directed there, my guides were talking to me telepathically telling me to get *him* to edit my book.

I went on to tell Carl that I had just arrived to the area and I wrote books with a group of Pleiadians. I was looking for an editor for my newest book, *The Sacred Contract: The Accounts of a Pleiadian Traveler*.

Not being a stranger to the metaphysical and the Masters, Carl thoughtfully advised me, "You should discuss it with your guides and find out if we are to work together."

I smiled and stated, "I already have. We would like you to edit my book."

After that was said, Carl told me he was moving to another house, hence the yard sale. It would take a while before he would be able to get to the job. No matter, I *thought,* a couple of weeks tops and we will fly on this. I can wait.

Since this agreement was made, I have waited for over five months to get my manuscript back from Carl. He has had one thing after another come up making it impracticable to impossible for him to work on my manuscript.

While patiently waiting for something to shift with the edit, Carl has been instrumental in connecting me with other people in the area. I was impressed enough to wait a little longer for him to get to my project.

Finally, Carl was caught up with his formatting and edits for other authors and was ready to begin on my book. His target completion date was in two weeks. I was on cloud nine. Even so, I tried not to get too excited. I had heard him speak of other projects he had done and how he thought it would take one week but ended up taking two or three weeks instead.

As I continued to wait for my book to be edited a knot began to grow in my stomach. Perhaps it was the excitement that *The Sacred Contract* was finally going to be ready for print! But I suspected there were more to it. I knew fear was settling in—that something else may get in the way postponing yet again this step in finishing my book.

A week after the expected completion date, I received an e-mail from his companion saying that Carl had had a bike wreck. They were working to get him healed. Unfortunately, he was unable to work.

Later I learned he had broken several bones—bones that could not be immobilized with a cast. *Now what?*

Three weeks passed with me hearing tidbits of information here and there concerning what modalities of healing they had chosen and Carl's progress. Of course my book was on hold…again.

Emotionally, I was frustrated and felt utterly powerless.

✳ ✳ ✳

I was given a week and then I was to go to Carl to tell him I wanted my book back finished or not. My father, Quem had come to me directly with the command, "Go to Carl next Monday and request to have your book given back to you."

I was stunned, afraid to act. For days, I sat with my father's directive not knowing how to proceed. My father who was usually upfront may be testing me to use my heart to make my decision. Intellectually, I thought there may be more information that would come through. Just sitting with his directive and purposefully choosing not to make any presumptions, I waited until I had more to go on.

As the days went by, though, I realized that what Carl and I shared was a business venture and if someone isn't upholding their end of the bargain then there is no business! One simply cannot wait indefinitely on someone to produce no matter what the circumstances are.

Monday came and as directed, I made the phone call to go visit Carl, although I hadn't made a commitment to take back my book. I wanted to talk with Carl, see him and be the judge myself deciding if I should get the book back then or wait a few more days.

At the front door, I was greeted by Carl's companion and was directed to slip off my shoes before I entered. I could clearly see Carl lying in a recliner on the other side of the living area next to a large picture window. He had an unobstructed view of Mt. Shasta that was spectacular. As I approached Carl I noticed he looked rather pale, a bit thinner and had grown a full beard.

The visual of Carl lying flat on his back was reminder enough to center myself and watch my thoughts, emotions, and how I spoke. I was to be compassionate no matter where the conversation took us. He was vulnerable and needed complete rest. For a fast recovery, he was to remain as immobile as possible in a positive space, not only in his home (physically), but mentally, emotionally, and spiritually as well. More than anything I wanted the conversation to be upbeat—uplifting giving him hope and motivation to continue his healing process.

The Book, *The Sacred Contract,* in the big scheme of things, was still after all just a book. People are more important than things.

At first, we discussed issues surrounding his healing and how that process was affecting his work. I was well aware that when anyone undergoes something this significant he is being given an opportunity to review all aspects of his life. In other words, it is *the* time to do inner-work—a time to review his life—time for reflection.

Throughout the conversation, I was telepathically reminded to get the book back. I ignored the promptings and allowed the conversation to flow and take us where Spirit directed.

Finally, I decided to honor Quem's directive and shifted the conversation a bit to explain to Carl that Quem had come and spoken to me; that he had directed me to get the book back.

Carl's facial expression changed. I saw his manner shift as well. Carl knows who Quem is. In Carl's voice, I heard a deep respect as he quickly stated that he should give me the book back at least for me to accept or reject his proposed corrections. I hesitated.

Intuitively, I knew that Carl wanted to finish the job. Logically, I thought it was impossible. Carl went on to say maybe they could rig up some sort of table so he could remain in a reclined position as he edited.

In the end, I left Carl's home and *The Sacred Contract,* saying, "I'll give you a few more days to see if you can figure out a way to work on the book or not."

That evening I prayed for healing for Carl. Then I asked that Stephanó go to his side and assist him. All at once I saw that even though this was a business deal, my heart had opened up allowing me to see and feel more than one side to the equation. Stephanó didn't pause to think about my request. He quickly replied, "I will leave at once!"

I then heard Franklin (Stephanó's assistant) assure me, "I will remain by your side. Your healing sessions will continue."

✳ ✳ ✳

Three days has passed since Stephanó left for Carl's house to assist him. No communication has taken place between Carl, Stephanó, and myself. Father Quem has remained silent concerning the book even though I have asked for more guidance.

PART
SEVEN

A CHANGE IN GUIDES

CHAPTER
TWENTY-NINE

Nathanal reminded me that it was lunch time. "Nakala! Go take care of your needs." Reluctantly, I pushed my chair away from my desk and swiveled it allowing me room to stand up. As I stood up I noticed that I had grown a bit stiff. Thanking Nathanal for his diligence, I walked out of the office to heat up some water for tea and then I headed directly for the bathroom. As I was in the middle of "taking care of my needs," as Nathanal politely puts it, I heard someone announce, "I am to write with you today. This is Monteró."

I groaned out loud and thought, so much for privacy. "Well," I began, "this is all nice and good but don't you think this is an odd time to announce your intention?" I felt a little annoyed to have my space invaded like that.

Just a few days earlier, I had heard someone introduce themselves to me as Monteró. At the time, he didn't tell me who he was or why he had come—he had simply made the introduction. I didn't think on it much as there were so many changes taking place at the same time and some of them were concerning guidance. To put it bluntly, I was overcome with all the new guides that had been making their selves known. Monteró hadn't been the only one. It seemed highly likely that a new writer was being lined up.

Impromptu, I had enrolled for a night class in business development and begun working with a local woman to redesign and update my business card. My days had become extremely busy to the point that I was feeling overwhelmed. In addition, I was acutely aware that Babaró prepared to take his leave. I was to have new guidance. That was just the tip of the iceberg.

Lately, I had begun to recognize feelings of vulnerability, like the rug was about to be pulled out from under me. I was struggling to stay centered. I wanted to take on a wait-and-see attitude concerning Babaró's position. I had learned all too well not to presume anything.

I worked to sooth my nerves by addressing this new guide who had shown up, Monteró. From past experience I reasoned he may be an overseer, doing assessments, visiting, or he may be gearing up to teach me in some way. At the time of his introduction, Monteró did not attempt to engage me in idle chit chat. On the side, I had speculated that Monteró was of the Akasie family as Monteró, though spelled differently also happens to be Quem's middle name.

Slowly, I took a sip of Jasmine tea and felt the warmth fill my body and ease the tension that had accumulated from my speculations.

Sensing that Monteró stood near I easily felt his energy. Intuitively I knew that he was ready to begin his transmission. He was more than ready to begin.

Monteró responded to my thought, "Yes, that is fact. I am ready to commence with our dialogue. However, before we get into it. I remind you that it is lunch time. A hot beverage does not suffice."

Inwardly, I chuckled, "Okay, I will take some time and get a real meal."

"See that you do," Monteró had said in a tone that indicated he was in full command.

I shook my head, taking note that this guy, whoever he was, meant business.

* * *

After a 'real' lunch, I laid down on the couch for a while to allow Franklin to assist me in resetting my energy. I was looking at a long day ahead of me. Tonight was the first night of my business class. I wanted to be well rested so I would retain the information presented.

After my short respite, I went out to stand on the front porch to feel the sunshine on my body and breathe in some fresh air before I sat down to receive.

As I sat down I announced out loud, "I am ready." Nothing happened. I waited a moment and then began to feel this wonderful vibration start in my calves travel up through my body. It felt so good that I thought I may cry. Then the energy turned cold and my digestive track began to gurgle. Ick, it sounded like it was in distress. As suddenly as the sound had begun it stopped.

Another wave of pure love went through my body and my breath caught.

"I announced myself just then," Monteró said, "As I am ready to commence. I am your master, the one you have been waiting for. I am to teach you the ways of energy: to control and direct energy. Your God-Self—your I Am Presence, has waited for eons to reveal Its Presence and express Itself in entirety through the flesh body—the one you see when you look in a mirror. You are to call me, Master." I nodded my head affirming that I understood as I wondered what exactly lay before me.

"Master Babaró has stepped away from your teaching. He will not return during your present embodiment. He has decided and been granted to reincarnate. He is totally involved in that endeavor. A family in the Midwest has been selected. Perhaps one day you will meet him—speak with him face to face."

"But," I began, then suddenly stopped not knowing if it was acceptable to interrupt, "Babaró assured me he would stay on until this book was finished."

"Ah, know it. The book is finished. We just channel it through you."

A wave of sadness moved through me. Remorse crept in, "I wanted to at least say good bye." Monteró didn't respond.

"We move on. As Master, to you, I direct your teachings. You have asked for discipline in order to train the ego to not react to any comments or cues. The training isn't an easy one but in order to ascend the ego must be dealt with in entirety. Healing must be complete on all levels. You are to be free of all blocks thus allowing God to work through the lower mind directing your endeavors entirely for service to all. You have, in earnest, asked for training to take you to the fifth dimensional consciousness. This, for you, I am to accomplish. I am your Master."

In the past few weeks, I had noticed a marked increase in discipline; my days were more regimented including more times to receive healing energy and meditate. Daily, now, I was receiving messages from specific Ascended Masters.

In addition, the more mundane tasks were dealt with easily as Nathanal, my twin flame, bless his heart, had taken over with planning meals, choosing what clothing I was to wear, when to clean and do laundry, and when to shop or run errands. You name it, he had it figured out when to do things and how more easily to accomplish. My meals were now gluten and sugar-free and totally healthy, except for the tortilla chips that I still ate on occasion.

Even though I saw my daily tasks taken care of, when hearing the Master's words, I had to be honest: I felt a ripple of fear like a jagged piece of glass cut through me.

What Master Monteró said was true. I had asked for these teachings. In all sincerity, I had asked. I had the faith that I would receive the teachings even though I had not known how or when.

Suddenly, I paused from typing and thought about it all—the implications of what I faced. My thoughts raced ahead. Time for myself, just to relax, had become a rare occasion and a notable twinge of sorrow sweep through me. Then I heard, "This is a time for rejoicing. This is no time for doubt, fear, or regrets! You are taking—accepting responsibility. No longer are you to allow your ego to direct you in your thoughts or your dealings with humanity—your God-Self has been appointed to fully illuminate Itself through the physical body directing you forward."

✳ ✳ ✳

As I stood to go ready myself for my evening class in Mt. Shasta, my phone signaled that I had received an e-mail. Curious I pushed the buttons to retrieve the message. It was from Carl. I saw the paperclip icon indicating there was an attachment. Abruptly, I sat back down to the computer to open the e-mail to open the attachment. Just as I opened the file the phone rang. The caller ID said it was Carl. Excitement, gratitude, disbelief, and relief all wrapped up into one, surfaced. I answered the phone and heard Carl's voice come through. "I wanted to make sure you knew that I had sent the book back. I finished it."

My heart pounded with excitement, gratitude, and love as I recalled my prayer that Carl be healed, I exclaimed, "Oh, My God!"

As I gained my composure a bit, I was able to ask Carl, "What happened?" Carl answered, his voice strong, unwavering, "I was able to work without distraction. Everything flowed perfectly. I had clarity."

I am not sure what happened there, but obviously someone or something has been working in our favor.

CHAPTER
THIRTY

A few days ago, Master Monteró gave me a message making it crystal clear that he expected me to rise earlier every morning: 6:30 to be exact. "It is time that you discipline yourself a little more. With that action," he added, "you are allowing yourself more moments that are just for you. This is a great gift. You will find yourself in a peaceful state all day. In essence, you are setting a specific tone by allowing yourself more time in a relaxed manner before your work-day begins."

"You have noticed that when you sleep later, even thirty minutes later, you create an energy that is hurried to get things done so you may sit at your desk and begin your writings. This is not helpful to your being."

"Today you made it a point to get up as you had agreed to. The result has been most pleasurable. The early hours of the morning were uninterrupted; the flow pristine."

* * *

The writing of this book has slowed down considerably. I have heard several times that the book is nearly complete—finished. Even so, I am not ready to step away from this book, for what I do is dearest to my heart. When I finally do lay down the writing my energy will be on other activities that are associated with being an author: things that I find challenging and possibly not as rewarding. I will not be doing what I find comfortable and what I do best.

Thoughts of being challenged by the steps in front of me overtake as getting the book formatted, printed, creating a cover, and selling the book come into play, overriding my contentment as a writer. These are areas that I have not excelled in. Feelings of disappointment and anxiety come into play, like neon gray-green ooze that is spreading over my body, seeping into the pores and eating my flesh.

My situation is quite ironic. I should be happy, feeling a great measure of satisfaction for what I have accomplished thus far.

The image of this ugly matter spreading over my body isn't at all pretty and is a reminder of how fast we can sabotage our soul's purpose and fall into feelings of self-pity.

The ooze is a symbol of negative thoughts and how they spread, always ugly and unwanted—a poison that must be eradicated. I can easily be consumed by these thoughts and feelings if I do not act now!

It is time that I shift out of that state of mind—feeling sorry for myself and with determination moving into a state of gratitude and empowerment. Only then may I go forward into an expanded state of awareness serving the people here on this Earth for the highest good and get on with the other steps of getting a book published and out in the hands of my audience.

Still, I would much rather offer these tasks to someone else who excels in those areas.

"Nakala," I heard, "you understand that you do not wish to take on these segments of this project because you are not yet proficient at them. Presently these tasks are a challenge for you: you are not comfortable in even beginning them. When you become acquainted and proficient with the process of each step you will find a deep satisfaction in your newly acquired skills and a sense of accomplishment that you were disciplined enough to carry through with it all!

"It is much like the writing process, you had to stick to it—be committed to work on the writing every day—continue forth, even though in the beginning, you were not the best writer and even now you are able to see room for improvement. Does this detour you?"

I understood what Master Monteró was saying, but with the writing I was totally into it. I wanted, more than anything else, to write! Now, there are these other pieces to it that I would just as well let someone else take care of. There are so many areas that a writer must excel in in order to get their books out. It all seems a bit frustrating and even overwhelming to me.

Master Monteró cut in, "May I remind you that you are to keep your eye on the prize but stay in this moment—BE in this moment. Don't jump ahead. Stay centered—balanced. There will be no thoughts and feelings of being over-burdened and fearful that you will not achieve.

"Many get to this point in the writing process and feel that there are too many steps to get the books printed and sold. You have been told time and again that you are being guided with each step."

Master Monteró then shifted the subject a bit as he began his teaching. "You remember your move here from Shawnee, Kansas?"

"Yes, I do."

"You were told to allow Nathanal to plan each step. He would tell you what you were to work on and when you were to complete that step. You were not even to look at what else you needed to do."

"Master Monteró, thinking back on the preparation for that move and even the move itself brings such a flood of emotions. During that time everything fell into place. I am not going to say everything had been perfect, but it was all laid out and executed with precision!"

In a soothing tone Master Monteró counseled, "The same is to occur here with the publishing and distribution of your books. To assist you in becoming familiar with the business side of being an author, you are taking a class. This means homework. To assist you in the marketing and distribution aspects of the business you have united with area authors to create a catalog to market your books. This means each person takes to the table what they are good at and implements those skills.

"In the meantime, you have the books to continue on with. I say, create segments to each day, allocating a certain amount of time on each project through the week. Parcel out the work load."

* * *

I couldn't help myself, the tears turned on. I felt a great outpouring of grief that this portion of the project had come to a finish. I sensed

Monteró standing near waiting for me to calm myself before he continued with his say. With all of my mind and my heart I willed him not to say anything! But it wasn't to be. I took a deep breath and then another before he moved into alignment and spoke.

"Nakala, it is time that we close this book. We have accomplished what we have set out to. You have a new staff (team) to familiarize yourself with. New teachings come with new guides and masters. Perhaps in the near future another volume of *The Accounts of a Pleiadian Traveler* will present itself."

CONCLUSION

Only a few days passed before I heard the title to the next volume in *The Accounts of a Pleiadian Traveler—The Fifth Sphere: Attainment*. The title brings forth a feeling of accomplishment, a completion of sorts.

Although, I know that with any ending there is a new beginning. Be assured that the Beings of Light who desire to bring forth the teachings continue on. Never do they give up.

With each book that is brought through me I feel such a wave of gratitude. I know that the books are meant as much for you as me. Through the channeled writings and dictations, as some call them, I receive hope, insights that inevitably lead to healing on some level—freedom—a way to let go. I sincerely hope that you too, receive the gift that shows you the way home.

~Nakala

www.ingramcontent.com/pod-product-compliance
Lightning Source LLC
Chambersburg PA
CBHW070941190726
48292CB00004B/1294